The Deputy's Wife

The Deputy's Wife

ROBERT LANE

A Black Horse Western

ROBERT HALE · LONDON

Photoset in North Wales by
Derek Doyle & Associates, Mold, Flintshire.
Printed and bound in Great Britain by
WBC Book Manufacturers Limited, Bridgend.

ONE

'Only the good die young.' Sheldon King pushed into the discussion as he sat at a table in Bronco Ashurst's saloon. He was having a quiet drink with the town dentist, Dennis Eames.

'There are plenty of markers up on Boot Hill to dispute that,' Eames reminded him.

The sixty-year-old saddler with the down-turned mouth in a plump face and heavy jowls was reluctant to be denied. 'All the same, my money says Jenkins'll live longer than Urquart. Titus is a square-shooter an' I'll allow he's good with a gun, but he ain't no match for Jenkins.'

'You think it'll come to that . . . a shoot-out?'

King's eyebrows arched and his high forehead furrowed. 'You see any other outcome to a situation like this? You mark my words, Den, Jenkins'll head straight for Eden as soon as he's released.'

Eames, still bright-eyed even though his full head of hair was greying now, was a few years younger than the saddler and had a far more engaging personality.

He scratched his pepper and salt, well-trimmed beard and observed, 'He's already on his way then. He was released this morning.'

'How come you know that?'

'Sheriff told me.'

'He tell you he was expectin' trouble?'

'I got the impression he's prepared for it.'

Eames took a pull on his beer.

Eyes firmly fixed on his companion, King said, 'Ten years in the county jail won't have made Jenkins any more amiable. Beats me what Wilhelmina ever saw in him.'

'She was still young and naive twelve years ago. She's grown up since then. Acquired more sense.'

King scoffed. 'You tryin' t'tell me that marryin' a deputy makes good sense?'

The dentist shrugged. 'I guess you've gotten a point there, what with all the risks of her becoming a widow any day. Being a lawman is a dangerous business, but I guess she preferred to be married to a man who upholds the law instead of that outlaw, after she got her divorce.'

'High ideals is one thing: havin' t'put on widow's weeds is another.'

'Wilhelmina has been married to Titus for more than five years now and he's never had so much as a scratch,' Eames reminded the saddler.

'I'll allow he's good at his job, but his luck'll run out one day. Tomorrow, maybe, when Jenkins gets here.'

Eames favoured King with a grin. 'You've no proof

8

he'll head this way. He'll know the sheriff and his deputy will be watching for him. Besides, he may not give a damn about Wilhelmina divorcing him. He could always get any woman he wanted.'

They both looked towards the batwings as Titus Urquart stood for a moment with a hand on each, holding them half open, gazing around the saloon. The deputy took in the dozen men scattered at the bar and the tables, nodded briefly at the saddler and the dentist, then turned to leave, apparently satisfied that no trouble was likely to disturb the normal tranquillity of a Monday evening in Eden.

After he had gone, Sheldon King said, 'He looks kinda worried, wouldn't you say?'

'Cautious, more like. Prepared, just in case. Even if Jenkins does come back and even if he takes the train, it won't get in till nine o'clock.'

'If he don't use the train he'll have t'buy a horse an' saddle an' I doubt he has the money for that, comin' straight from the county jail.'

Again, Eames fixed his gaze on the saddler. 'But we both know that would be no problem to a man like Jenkins. He could have money within an hour of his release.'

'You're forgettin', Den, they confiscated his gunbelt an' weapon when they arrested him.'

Eames found it hard to believe the saddler could be so naive. 'How long do you think it would take him to replace them?'

Suitably chastened, King acknowledged that a man as ruthless as Duane Jenkins could scare the living daylights out of any store owner who sold weapons and gunbelts, without having to kill him.

County Sheriff Kirk Nazeby sat at his desk, immaculately combed hair prematurely white, forehead lined, strong jaws still retaining most of his teeth, studiously thoughtful. He looked up as Titus Urquart opened the door and entered, his eyes questioning.

'Town's as quiet as the grave, Sheriff.'

'No talk about Jenkins?'

'Didn't hear any.'

Nazeby was not surprised. Folks would be nervous about mentioning the outlaw to the man who had married his former wife.

'Did you tell Wilhelmina that her ex-husband could be on his way back here?'

'No. He might not come, so why get her all worked up about something that maybe won't happen?'

'Then again it might. If he's coming and he takes the train he could be here tonight. We'll go down to the depot later and wait for it. I want to know where that bastard is. He could be after me as well as you.'

Urquart slanted a thoughtful gaze towards the sheriff. 'You mean because it was you who captured him?'

'Right. He's a nasty piece o' work, that Duane Jenkins. He never said anything after his trial, but I could read his mind.'

'Didn't you tell me he never killed anyone except in self-defence?'

'That's a fact, far as I know, but ten years can

10

change a man. Jenkins is not the forgiving kind and he's the fastest man with a gun I ever set eyes on.'

'Faster than me?'

'I reckon. You're good, Titus, which is why I wanted you as my deputy, but I wouldn't bet money on you to beat Jenkins in a showdown.'

'Well I'll tell you one thing, Sheriff ... if he attempts to go anywhere near my wife the question should soon be settled.'

Except for the light glowing from the depot office the track was veiled in darkness. Titus Urquart did not need to ask why so many of the townsmen were lounging around as if they were waiting to catch the train. Only two of them were actually toting baggage, intending to board for points north.

It was normal for either the sheriff or his deputy to meet the night train, just to make a note of any strangers coming to town, but usually there were no more than a half-dozen of Eden's citizens taking any interest. The women were customarily at home, apart from the saloon girls, and the men were slaking their thirst, some of them trying their luck at the gaming tables. Judging by the number of them waiting expectantly, the saloons must be half empty, Urquart surmised. This sudden interest meant only one thing: they were waiting to see if Duane Jenkins came back to town. And if he did, what would he do?

Time seemed to drag for most of them as never before, but more particularly for Sheriff Nazeby and his deputy. Impatience was high by the time they heard the engine whistle blow.

'Well, we'll soon know,' one of the townsmen muttered softly.

Urquart walked away from Nazeby as planned, to give them a better chance of observing who got off the train. It slowed some distance before reaching the depot and seemed to take an age to grind to a halt and let out a jet of steam.

Urquart could barely remember what Duane Jenkins looked like. It had been so long since he had seen the outlaw and, at the time, Urquart was working as a cowhand on one of the ranches in the county. He had not even known Wilhelmina Jenkins then, but after her husband had been sent to prison he had encountered her for the first time and been deeply smitten. One look into those dark-brown eyes had been enough, but added to that was the full mouth set in a face that was crowned with jet-black hair. She was beautiful. He had known instantly that he wanted her. He knew that other men lusted after her, but he was prepared to offer her a wedding ring, whereas the others were somehow too scared to make a commitment that might bring them a bullet once Jenkins had served his time. And there was always the chance that he might escape a lot sooner and come gunning for any man who even looked at Wilhelmina sideways. Even Duane Jenkins had been obliged to marry her to get what he wanted and keep other suitors at bay. A sixteen-year-old virgin was a prized possession for any man.

Recollections flashed through Urquart's mind as

he had waited for the train to enter the depot and disgorge its passengers.

At first he had not known how to approach her, bearing in mind that she was still a married woman. The chance had come when the roof on her house had started to leak and his employer, who happened to be Wilhelmina's uncle, had sent him to patch it up. She had been wary of him at first, knowing how men lusted after her, but her uncle had assured her she had nothing to fear from Titus Urquart. She told him later that as soon as she saw him looking at her with adoring eyes she knew what was in his mind.

'You were about as different to Duane as any man could be. You looked at me with love in your eyes, not lust. I knew before I met him that Duane was a ladies' man, but like every other woman, I thought I could change him. Only I wasn't really a woman at the time, even though I thought I was. I didn't know then that he made a living robbing banks.'

She did not say that Duane Jenkins was a hand-some man and that part of the difference between them was the fact that Titus had a plain, almost hang-dog face that would hardly fascinate a woman. To Jenkins she had been a possession, a woman who adored him and was blind to his failings and there-fore easily manipulated. It was Titus Urquart's down-right honesty and profession of love that had won her hand when he suggested she divorce her jailbird spouse and marry him.

'He'd kill us both when he came out if I did,' she warned.

'According to the sheriff he's never actually killed any man, except in self-defence.'

'There's always a first time, Titus. He's a very proud and possessive man.'

'You can't still love him, after what he's done!'

'No, not any more. I thought I did. I was only sixteen when we married. I was living with my uncle out at the ranch, just before you came here, and I ran off with Duane without telling anyone, because we knew Uncle would try to stop us.'

Urquart came back to the present with a start. The conductor was shouting 'All aboard!' as memories braked to a halt and Urquart noticed only three passengers had alighted from the train. Two of them were a man and his wife Urquart knew well. The third was a tall man carrying a single bag in his right hand. In the dark it was difficult to distinguish his features, but when Urquart saw the sheriff move towards him he knew that the man was Duane Jenkins. Why would a right-handed gunman put himself at a disadvantage by carrying his luggage in that hand instead of his left?

And then Urquart noticed something quite unexpected when the outlaw and the sheriff faced each other as light from the depot office brought them into clearer focus.

There was no gunbelt on Jenkins' hip.

TWO

The men standing in groups alongside the rails as the train pulled out watched and waited expectantly as Titus Urquart walked slowly towards Duane Jenkins and the sheriff. The outlaw and the county sheriff had halted and stood facing each other.

'So you've come back, Jenkins. You're not welcome, so I suggest you make your stay no longer than one night.'

Duane Jenkins' lips curled in a sneer. 'Well, if it ain't Kirk Nazeby, an' still wearin' that star.' He shook his head as if in disbelief. 'I'd'a thought some gunny woulda put a couple o' bullets in you before now.'

'Eden is still a peaceful town and I've gotten me a deputy fast enough with a gun to scare off the hoodlum element we get passing through here from time to time.'

Urquart drew near enough to hear Jenkins' response.

'Now would that be the one who stole my wife?'

'She is not your wife any more, Jenkins, so you just forget about her and move on.'

15

'The man ain't been born who could forget about Wilhelmina. Hell, Nazeby, ain't she the most beautiful woman you ever did see? She ain't been out o' my mind in ten years.'

'But she is not your woman any more, Duane. You know damn well she divorced you and remarried. She's happy with her new husband, so get that through your thick skull.'

Jenkins let out an exaggerated sigh. 'It's been a long day an' that badge don't entitle you t'tell me what t'do, Sheriff, an' I need a bed. See you in the mornin', if you're lucky.'

He passed Nazeby and Urquart joined the sheriff. Together they watched him go as the townsmen started to follow.

'He'll go to the hotel tonight,' Nazeby told Urquart, 'but there's no telling what's in his mind, so you get back to that wife of yours and stay with her.'

'I guess I'd best do that.'

'And don't shirk the issue. You tell her Jenkins is back before somebody else does.'

The two lawmen eyed each other in silence, until Urquart said, 'I'll tell her in the morning. No reason to spoil her sleep tonight.'

But Sheriff Nazeby had been wrong about what Duane Jenkins would do immediately he had left the depot and headed towards the hotel. Instead of going inside he walked on by, in the direction of the house he had shared with Wilhelmina. There was

16

light inside the closed, draped windows and he wondered who was in residence. He felt confident that Deputy Sheriff Urquart would not have been agreeable to living in the house his divorced wife had shared with him, so who could it be? Someone he knew or strangers?

He opened the gate in the white picket fence, glad to know it had been kept in good repair during his absence, and approached the door. He didn't bother to knock and turned the door handle, which moved easily in his hand. He went inside, to face a woman who got up out of a basket wing-chair, alarm in the gaze she fixed on him.

'Who are you? What do you want? My husband is out. You'll have to come back tomorrow.'

There was something familiar about her that set Jenkins trying to place her, but recognition dawned in her eyes before his.

She gasped with surprise, but her fear evaporated. 'You're Duane Jenkins.'

'Now fancy you rememberin' me. You must have been just a kid when I went away. You've grown into a very charmin' and beautiful woman.'

'Flatterer. I've got enough sense to know that I'm not at all beautiful. Everybody said you could charm the birds off the trees and, yes, I suppose I was a kid when you were captured. I'm Celeste Winchmore, Celeste Smith as was, and I was thirteen the last time I saw you.'

'Not the butcher's daughter?'

'The same, but I think you should leave now, Mr

17

The Deputy's Wife

Jenkins. My husband wouldn't like to find you here with me.'

He favoured her with his most winning smile. 'But this is my house, Celeste.'

'Not any more. My husband bought it from your former wife.'

He laughed softly. 'Wilhelmina had no authority to sell it, Celeste, so he wasted his money; legally, you an' your husband are trespassin'.'

As he continued to charm her with his smile she felt his male magnetism and began to understand how he had attained his reputation with women.

He broke the brief silence by saying, 'But we can sort all that out in the mornin'. I need somewhere to lay my head until then. I've had a tirin' day, so I'll use the bed in what was originally intended as the nursery. When your husband comes home, tell him we'll discuss the problems in the mornin'. Or is there not a bed in the spare room?'

'I'm afraid our daughter is asleep in there.'

'Your daughter! And how old would she be?'

'Three.'

'Then you have a choice, Celeste: either take her in with you tonight or I'll take your room. Which is it to be?'

The sound of people approaching penetrated the walls of the house and she looked towards the door, delaying her answer. The door burst open and a man in his early thirties came through in a hurry, fear in his eyes.

In the silence that stretched while the two men

18

eyed each other, the one in apprehension, Jenkins calmly weighing him up, Celeste Winchmore made the introductions.

'This is my husband, Philip, Mr Jenkins.'

Jenkins remembered Philip Winchmore and knew he offered no threat. The man had always been a coward, too scared to carry a gun in case he got drawn into a confrontation and had to use it.

Sheriff Nazeby barged in moments later, gun in hand.

Duane Jenkins glared at him. 'Put that gun away, Sheriff. Neither Mr Winchmore nor me are armed an' this is none o' your business.'

Winchmore said querulously, 'What are you doing here with my wife?'

'We were discussin' where I'm gonna sleep t'night, so now you can have your say.' Jenkins switched his gaze back to the sheriff. 'An' that don't concern you, Sheriff, so git!'

Nazeby looked at Celeste. 'He been bothering you, Celeste?'

'No, Sheriff, not at all, and I think it would be best if you left me and Philip to sort this out ourselves. As Mr Jenkins pointed out, he is not wearing a gun, so we shall be quite safe.'

They could hear murmurs through the open doorway from the men gathered outside, curious to know what was happening in the house, but not venturing too close, aware of the fearsome reputation of Duane Jenkins.

'You sure about that?'

'Yes, Sheriff, I'm quite sure.'

Her husband objected. 'Now hold on a minute. I want this man out of here and if it takes the sheriff to get rid of him. . . .'

'It's all right, Philip. We can sort this out ourselves.' She looked back at Nazeby. 'Goodnight, Sheriff, and thank you for your concern.'

Hesitantly the sheriff looked from her to her husband, then at Jenkins, before holstering his gun. 'In that case. . . .'

He turned and went outside, closing the door behind him. They heard him call to the mob. 'On your way now. This is none of your concern. Get back to your own homes.'

Celeste Winchmore explained to her husband what Jenkins had told her concerning the ownership of the house, which made him bridle immediately.

'I paid good money for this house and now it's mine, no matter what you say.'

'I'm not gonna argue with you about that t'night, Winchmore. All you have t'decide right now is where I'm gonna sleep.'

Celeste said quickly, seeing her husband was on the point of objecting, 'We'll take Chloe in with us, Philip, and Mr Jenkins can have her bed.'

'Why should we? Why can't he get a bed at the hotel?'

'Because I prefer to sleep in my own home,' Jenkins answered for her. 'Now, just use your head and do as your wife suggests.'

Winchmore had always avoided trouble of any sort, particularly where violence was involved, and now he sensed the menace in the quiet voice, coupled with the steely glint in the outlaw's eyes, and his objections collapsed as his stomach churned in a return of fear.

Celeste turned to their visitor and asked, 'Would you like something to eat, Mr Jenkins? Coffee, maybe?'

'That's mighty civil of you, Celeste. Thank you.'

In spite of his qualms, Philip Winchmore was relieved by the politeness with which he spoke to Celeste. Maybe Jenkins was not the heartless villain he had been painted? Their two paths had seldom crossed before the outlaw had been captured and Winchmore's knowledge of Jenkins was based on hearsay only. Nevertheless, he was not going to give up the home he had purchased in good faith to a man who had just spent ten years in prison for bank robbery. He felt quite certain the law would back him up if the need should arise.

Wilhelmina Urquart looked squarely into her husband's eyes. 'Did you know he was on his way back here?'

The deputy had changed his mind about keeping his wife in the dark until morning.

'No, but we knew . . .'

'We?'

'Me and the sheriff. We knew he was due for release from jail this morning and the sheriff figured

21

it was possible he might come back here. Kirk suspected he might come gunning for him.'

'Because it was the sheriff who captured and gave evidence against him?'

'Right.'

She put her hands on her hips, adopting the stance of some outraged wife who had just been insulted.

'The sheriff knows very well Duane is no killer. Bank robber, yes, but he never shot a single soul in any of his robberies.'

'How can you be sure of that? You didn't even know he was robbing banks until they caught him.'

It was a fact she had to acknowledge to herself; but she was reluctant to back down. 'Duane was well known as an expert with guns, but he's not a gunslinger. Do you seriously think he would gun down the sheriff?'

'A man has a lot o' time to think in jail, Wil. He won't be the same man he was when he went in.'

'Well, if he's changed so much, why is he here? He knows very well I divorced him and married you.'

He looked back at her through a long silence.

Her voice dropped almost to a whisper as she read what was running through his mind. 'You think he's come back for me?'

She began to tremble and sat down heavily as her legs turned to jelly.

THREE

Her eyes stared at her trembling hands for long moments, then she lifted them to look at her husband. 'What are we going to do, Titus?'

'I guess that depends on you, Wil.'

'Why me? Don't you have anything to say about it?'

He took his time before answering. 'I love you, Wil, you know that, but I'm not stupid. You've never felt the same about me as you did about him. If . . .'

'But I was little more than a child then!' she protested. 'I'm a grown woman now. You've given me what Duane never could.'

'And what is that?'

'Peace of mind. Companionship. You're always here for me. Duane was away half the time, planning and robbing banks and pretending he was away on legitimate financial business.'

He almost smiled, although smiling was not one of his natural habits. 'You mean you want to stay with me, even if he asks you to go back to him?'

'Of course I do, you blockhead!'

She got out of her chair and rushed into his arms.

'I love you, Titus. You're the kindest man I ever knew.'

An hour later, Duane Jenkins was sound asleep in Chloe Winchmore's bed, although he had found it a little too short to stretch full length. He had barred the door with a chair, even though he was fairly confident that Philip Winchmore was much too timid to come and shoot him in his sleep, even if he did have a gun hidden away.

In the main bedroom, the child had settled back to sleep between her mother and father, but they were both still wide awake. They began to talk in whispers.

'Why were you so affable with that outlaw, Celeste?'

'What else could I do?'

'You could have told him to leave.'

'I did, only he made it quite plain he intended to stay the night. I didn't want any trouble.'

'The sheriff would have ordered him out if you hadn't been so eager for him to stay,' he reminded her with perverse relish.

'I *wasn't* eager for him to stay, but even if the sheriff had made him go to the hotel, he'd have come back again in the morning.'

'What for?'

'He claims Wilhelmina Urquart had no authority to sell the house. He says it's still his and you wasted your money.'

'We'll see about that!' he retorted angrily.

24

'He has a reputation, Philip.'

'With women, you mean? I know all about that.'

'He's also known as a hard man. Others are afraid of him. He's killed men in gunfights.'

'I know that as well, only I'm not planning to face him with a gun. The man has to see reason. This is our home. Has been for five years. I'm not going to let him take it away from us.'

Sheriff Kirk Nazeby was uneasy. Jenkins was apparently intent on reclaiming that house as his own, in spite of Wilhelmina having sold it to Philip Winchmore in a perfectly legitimate deal. Why else had Jenkins not found himself a hotel bed? Nazeby sensed trouble he had not envisaged and, not too sure of the legal position, was at a loss to know what he could do about it.

Had Wilhelmina any right to dispose of the property without Duane's sayso? If not, Jenkins could turn the Winchmores out on to the street.

He cursed softly to himself. Minutes later he decided there was nothing he could do about it until trouble sparked into life. He undressed and got into bed.

Breakfast was an unusually quiet time in the Winchmore home and in that of the Urquarts. Sheriff Nazeby took his in the diner across the street from the jailhouse, knowing there were things to think about other than Duane Jenkins.

'Isn't it time you reported for duty?' Urquart's wife

queried, after she had washed the dishes and Titus showed no intention of leaving her at the usual time.

'Best if I stay with you this morning, don't you think?'

'You mean in case Duane comes here?'

'Why else?'

She wasn't sure if her first husband might prove a threat if she was left alone and it would be comforting to have Titus around if Duane did pay her a call. She could not visualize what he might have to say to her, but she guessed he would want the money she had got for their former home. It was safely deposited in the bank, left untouched because she knew Titus would want no part of it. He was a proud man and had struggled to provide a home for them on his meagre pay, but it was that pride she respected. She would gladly hand over the money to Duane and be thankful to be rid of the responsibility.

'That was a fine breakfast, Mrs Winchmore,' Jenkins told her as she cleared the table.

He looked at her husband, read the apprehension in his silent stare, and decided not to waste any more time.

'Now you listen to me, Winchmore, an' don't interrupt.' He coughed, blew his nose, then continued, 'I understand you bought this house from my wife, but she had no authority to sell it, so legally it still belongs t'me. For the time bein' you can stay here an' I'll go an' see her; find out what she did with the money. If she still has it, maybe we can work somethin' out, but first off I need a horse an' saddle, a gunbelt an' a weapon, You think you could get all o' those things for me on credit? I'd pay you back within the week.'

'On those terms, I guess I could. I'm not without respect in this town and my name is good for enough credit to cover what you need.'

'Best add a rifle an' saddle pouch t'that list.'

'All right.'

'Off you go then. I'll get your wife to fill me in with all the local gossip while you're gone.'

'You won't. . . ?'

Jenkins shook his head. 'Molest her? You don't know much about me, do you? I never needed to rape a woman in my life. They were all glad enough to have me service 'em, so just you go an' do what needs t'be done an' let's not waste any more time.'

Winchmore pushed back his chair and went to collect his hat. He looked into the kitchen, sombre-eyed, and told his wife he would not be long. After he had left, Jenkins heard little Chloe ask her mother if she could go out to play.

'You're going to play with Susan?'

'Yes. I promised.'

'Off you go then, and be good.'

Jenkins went to join her mother after he heard the door close.

'Did you hear my conversation with your husband?'

'Most of it.'

'You know what he was scared of?'

27

She looked at him with mixed feelings and ran a hand through hair the colour of rusted iron. His animal magnetism was something she had never experienced before and she felt her heart pumping harder in her chest. She couldn't help wondering what it was like to be loved by such a man, especially when she thought how her own husband had never managed to satisfy her sexual needs.

'I think so,' she replied softly.

'An' how about you? Are you scared I might rape you?'

'No, I don't think you're that kind of man.'

He moved closer and put his hands on her shoulders. She did not flinch, but her throat was suddenly dry.

'I haven't had a woman for ten years, Celeste. Right now I need you, an' he need never know.'

FOUR

'You must be Titus Urquart,' Jenkins said, when the deputy opened the door in response to his knocking.

Jenkins noticed Urquart had his gunbelt strapped around his waist, Smith & Wesson .44 nestling snugly on his right hip.

'And you're Duane Jenkins. What do you want?'

Jenkins met the blatant hostility resolutely. 'A few words with my wife.'

'She's not your wife any more and well you know it.'

'Let's not argue about the technicalities. Do I get t'see Wil or not?'

'If you've unfinished business. . . .'

'We have.'

'Best come inside then. I don't want the pair of you talking on the street.'

It was some relief to Urquart to see that Jenkins had come unarmed.

The house was smaller than the one Jenkins had built for himself and his young bride twelve years ago, but comfortably furnished. That would be

Wilhelmina's doing, he decided as she stood facing him in the middle of the main room. She was still beautiful and hardly looked twelve years older than when he had taken her as his child bride.

'Hello, Wil. How are you?'

'I'm fine, Duane, And you?'

'About as well as a man can be after spendin' ten years in the cooler, an' a mite annoyed with you. You sold my house without my sayso.'

'It seemed the right thing to do at the time. The money is safely lodged in the bank for you. I haven't spent a cent of it. We can go and get it for you any tine you feel like it.'

'Right now?'

The years in prison had put a few lines on his face, she noticed, but he was still a handsome man and there was no sign of grey in the dark-brown wavy hair.

'If you wish.'

She looked at Titus and he gave the slightest nod of approval.

'I'll get my coat.'

She left the room and the two men locked eyes.

Jenkins said, 'You took advantage of her while I was away, Urquart. I don't like that.'

Urquart's mouth formed a sneer and the tone of his voice when he responded was in keeping. 'Did you expect her to depend on charity for ten years while she waited for you to come back?'

Before Jenkins could answer, the woman returned and his jaws clamped shut. She could see the hostility the two men felt for each other and decided she must do what she could to end it.

'After we've settled this banking business, Duane, I don't ever want to see you again. I'm married to Titus now and there isn't room for the both of you in Eden, so what are your plans?'

'The first thing is t'remind you o' that promise you made twelve years ago: "till death do us part". That's how I remember it, an' I ain't dead yet, Wil.'

'And what about the one you made, Duane? "Forsaking all others"? You cheated on me with your lying and your fornicating and you can't deny it and expect me to believe you.'

Jenkins switched his gaze to Urquart. 'I think me an' Wil had best have this conversation in private, Deputy.'

'We've said all there is to say, Duane,' Wilhelmina told him.

'Oh, no, we ain't, not by a long way.'

'I told you about Titus and the divorce when I visited you in prison that last time. I made it plain enough I wasn't going to sit around waiting for you.'

Urquart cut in. 'You heard what my wife said, Jenkins, and she's right; there's no room for you in this town any more, so let's get this money business settled, then you can ride out.'

Jenkins was not easily discouraged. 'We'll go down to the bank, but I'll decide whether I go or stay, not you.'

Winchmore had chosen well and Jenkins was pleased with the look of the chestnut gelding with the white on the lower forelegs. The horse was seven years old, according to what Winchmore had been told, and when Jenkins checked the animal's teeth he saw no reason to doubt the statement. The saddle and bridle were new, the rifle was a Winchester '73, the pistol in the new holster a Colt .44 calibre. He would need a lot of practice with it before he could think of challenging that deputy sheriff, bearing in mind that Urquart had established a reputation as a fast gun. But challenge him he would, when he was ready and his old skills had returned. Ten years was a long time to be without a gun and he knew his speed and co-ordination would be sadly in decline. Time and practice would soon put that right. Whatever she might think now, Wilhelmina would come back to him once Titus Urquart was no longer around to support her.

'You did well, Winchmore.' Jenkins did not inform him that he now had money to settle up with him and was relying on the storekeeper to honour the privacy that was customary between men of the West. 'I'll settle up with you In a few days.'

'You'll be moving into the hotel today, will you?'

His eyes hardened as Jenkins said, 'You mean I ain't welcome in my own house no more?'

Winchmore's mouth had grown dry and with that gun now loaded and resting high on Jenkins' right thigh, fingers of fear crawled all over him. His reply was little more than a hoarse whisper. 'My daughter needs her own bed.'

'You willin' t'pay my hotel bill for a week or so?'

Winchmore gulped. 'You said you'd have money in a few days.'

'Has it not got into that thick head o' yours I might not be welcome at the hotel?'

Celeste had come from the kitchen to join them. She kept her eyes on Jenkins as she spoke to her husband. 'I think we can manage for a little while, Philip, until Mr Jenkins can get his affairs in order. By then I expect he'll be glad to move on.'

Jenkins faced her with a smile on his lips and said politely, 'Thank you, Celeste. That's mighty agreeable of you.'

The adoring look in his wife's eyes was plainly evident to Winchmore as she held the outlaw's gaze. The green-eyed god began to spread seedlings of hatred through him. What the hell had been going on between them while he had been out?

FIVE

He rode the chestnut away from Eden on the northern trail, intent on getting in some shooting practice as quickly as possible. He rightly guessed that neither Sheriff Kirk Nazeby nor his deputy would challenge him to a fight. Both men, he had concluded, were proud of their reputations as fair-minded upholders of the law and for either of them to provoke him into a gunfight would reflect badly on their integrity. But there could be drifters or even residents in Eden who might want to take advantage of his rustiness in gunplay, keen to make a name for themselves for killing a man notorious as a fast gun. He was not ready for that. With a few hours' practise under his belt he would feel more confident.

Four miles along the trail he steered the gelding into the brush that fronted timber away to his left, dismounted and hitched him to a tree.

He began by practising his draw with an empty gun, getting the feel of the weapon before making any attempt to shoot with it. It felt heavy in his hand at first, after all those years of not handling a pistol,

34

but after a while he began to sense the old smoothness coming back. His love affair with guns was beginning to reassert itself, until he was caressing the handle rather than grabbing at it. He loaded the gun, picked himself a target, and began to shoot. The first twenty shots were way off target, but after that his aim gradually improved.

In little more than an hour he had used up all the shells Philip Winchmore had bought for him. Perhaps as well, he decided. His arm was beginning to tire with all the unaccustomed exercise. He pushed the weapon into the holster, unbuckled the gunbelt, and stowed them both in a saddle-bag. He unhitched the horse and climbed into the saddle. When he arrived back in town he would slake his thirst and test the atmosphere. He wasn't sure how hostile the populace would be to his return, but in view of the fact that he had never attempted to rob the bank in Eden, maybe they would look upon him with more curiosity than hatred. Not one of them had ever lost a cent because of his activities. The businessmen had benefited from his patronage. Neither did he owe any man in town. There might be a husband whose wife he had seduced who still nursed a hatred, but other than that, who would have reason to resent his return? He could think of no one.

Sheriff Kirk Nazeby was sitting behind his desk studying the latest Wanted posters that had come with the morning mail, when his deputy came into the office.

'He's just ridden back into town, Sheriff, and gone into Bronco's saloon,' Urquart said. 'What do you want me to do?'

Steepled hands touched Nazeby's chin as he rested his elbows on the desk, while he considered his reply.

'You think you can go in there without picking a fight with him?'

'Any trouble between us'll come from him.'

'Then keep an eye on him. I want to know everything he does, so we can figure out what his intentions are.'

'Will do, Sheriff.'

He went out and closed the door, then strolled leisurely towards Bronco Ashurst's saloon. He pushed open the batwings and rapidly surveyed the interior, sensing the atmosphere of high tension building up inside.

Away to his right, leaning against the bar, a glass in his hand, Duane Jenkins noticed the deputy's arrival, but the man facing him had his back to the lawman and all his attention was centred on Jenkins. The stranger's hands hovered above twin-holstered guns and his voice was harsh as he continued the conversation that had apparently started moments before Urquart's arrival.

'Well, it's true, ain't it? You've gotten a rep as a fast gun, right?'

'I ain't totin' a gun, as you can well see,' Jenkins replied calmly, as his worst nightmare began to evaporate now that Deputy Urquart had arrived.

'But there ain't no denyin' you're Duane Jenkins, fast gun.'

'I'm Jenkins, but I guess you'll jest have t'wait t'see how fast I am with a hogleg.'

'I ain't of a mind t'wait, mister.' The stranger turned his attention to a man with a holstered gun away to Jenkins' left. 'You! Give him your gun!'

'Don't drag me into this, stranger. I'm a peaceable man.'

'Then what're you doin' totin' that weapon? Is it just for ornament?'

'I know which end the bullets come out of,' the townsman bridled, affronted.

'Then toss it to Jenkins, or we'll see just how good *you* are.'

Seeing how nervous Jesse Watt suddenly became, the deputy decided it was time for him to intervene. 'Gunfighters are not welcome in this town, mister, so. . . .'

The gunman whirled around to face Urquart, hands clutching at his weapons. Experience had taught the deputy that in similar situations there was no time to waste if he wanted to live. In the instant this stranger had his weapons leaping from leather, Urquart had his own gun levelled and spitting lead.

Jenkins watched the blur of hands with no time to take any evasive action, and then one gun clattered to the board floor, followed a moment later by the other, as the man who had wanted to enhance his own reputation as a fast gun was hurled backwards by Urquart's two bullets. Then the man's legs buckled and his body performed strange jerking movements as he slumped forward, hitting the floor face down.

Urquart kept his eyes on the dead man as he shucked the spent shells from his gun and replaced them before holstering it. The silence that had settled on the room was broken as the deputy lifted his eyes and faced Jenkins. 'Nobody told me your middle name is trouble.'

'You can't blame me for what happened. I only came in here to slake my thirst, Deputy.'

'And ran straight into trouble. We don't like trouble in Eden, as I believe the sheriff intimated last night.'

'I didn't start any trouble, like I told you.'

Jesse Watt piped up, 'But the deputy had to finish it, or either you or me could be lying dead on the floor instead of him.' He indicated the dead stranger lying perfectly still, then looked at Urquart. 'I don't know about Jenkins, Titus, but I'm mighty glad you arrived in time to put a stop to that lunatic.'

'You ever seen him before, Jesse?'

'No. Drifter, I reckon. He came in ten minutes before Jenkins. Soon as he heard the barkeep mention Jenkins' name he wanted to pick a fight.'

Sheriff Nazeby eased his way into the saloon, Colt pistol in his right hand. Assessing the situation at a glance, he put it back in its holster.

'I heard the shots and came running. You kill him, Titus?'

'Had no option, Sheriff. He wanted to kill Jenkins and, as you can see, he's not carrying.'

38

'It was self-defence, Sheriff,' Jesse Watt told him.

'I guess it must've been, Jesse, but thanks for the confirmation. Titus, go get Doc Hanson. We'd best get this troublesome stranger certified before we hand him over to Lew Pitchley for burial.'

As Urquart turned to leave, the sheriff faced Duane Jenkins. 'I guess I have to allow you didn't start this ruckus, Jenkins, but I'd be obliged if you'd move on. You're too much of an attraction to young gunnies wanting to try you out.'

'I might jest do that, Sheriff, after I've finished my business here in town.'

'Take you long, will it?'

'A week or two, I reckon.'

'I suggest you hurry it up some, 'less you plan to offer Lew the chance to sell another burying box.'

Phillp Winchmore came home to find Duane Jenkins sitting in his favourite chair and his resentment sparked into life again with added momentum. He had bought the old Jenkins house because Celeste had tired of living over the store in the middle of town. Now his idyllic life was being threatened by this womanizer who had already cast his spell over Winchmore's wife. Celeste greeted him with less than her usual warmth, but there was a spark in her eyes which had not been there two days ago. When she served up supper those eyes lit up each time they fixed on Duane Jenkins. The resentment in Winchmore rapidly built into hatred. Much as he loathed guns, if he had to kill this intruder to get his family life back to normal, then that was what he would do.

Immediately the practicalities of such action flared in his mind. Shooting him in the back with a handgun would get him arrested and charged with murder, even if he did claim that Jenkins had raped his wife, a charge he could not be sure was true and, even if it was, one that Celeste would doubtless deny. No, he had to be more subtle than that. A rifle shot from distance when Jenkins took one of his rides out of town would be much safer, but even that idea raised obstacles. Winchmore had never used a rifle in his life and he would need to get used to handling a long gun. How could he do that and keep the knowledge from both Jenkins and his wife?

How, indeed, could he persuade gunsmith Jay Nairn to keep quiet about the purchase of such a weapon? Jay would suspect some deep dark secret lay behind a sale of that significance. Just about everybody knew the storekeeper hated guns, which was why he had banned their sale from his store after his father died.

He decided he would have to tell Jay Nairn he was buying it for a friend as a surprise birthday present. Nairn had been quite satisfied when he had explained his purchases on behalf of the released prisoner, staying in his old home. He smiled with satisfaction as he cleaned up his plate as usual. His first problem was resolved.

Duane Jenkins did not notice the small smile on Winchmore's face as he ate more slowly than the storekeeper. After seeing the deputy sheriff in action earlier in the day he recognized he had problems of his own. Titus Urquart was the fastest man with a gun he had ever seen and he knew he would need a lot more practice if he was to get the better of him in a shoot-out. The deputy's reflexes were awesome.

SIX

Wilhelmina Urquart let out a small sigh of relief when she saw her husband come into the house. Her eyes swept over him as she offered him a welcoming smile. He was unharmed. The only blight on their marriage was the constant fear that one day he might be lying dead on the street, shot by some gun-toting maniac.

'I hear you had a little excitement today.'

'Can't a man keep anything quiet in this town?' he grumbled good-humouredly.

'Some things, I suppose, but not when you kill a gunslinger. That's news and they shout it from the housetops.' She checked the cookpots on the stove before turning back to him. 'One thing worries me though, Titus.'

'And what might that be?'

'They're now saying you're the fastest gun in the territory. Faster than Duane, even, and that means other gun-crazy men will be coming to Eden to test you out. I'm beginning to think all men are mad, wanting to prove themselves better than the next man, and killing a fellow human being doesn't even give them a twinge of conscience.'

Urquart knew he could not argue with that but he had to defend himself. 'You think I'm like that, Wil?'

She hurried to him and put her arms around his neck. 'No, Titus, I didn't mean you, but I don't want you to have to go on killing these madmen just so that you can stay alive.' She hugged him to her breast and pressed her cheek to his. 'Let's go away and start over some place where no one knows you.'

'Then folks would say I quit town because I was scared of Jenkins,' he protested.

'I don't care what they say! I want you safe. Widow's weeds wouldn't suit me.'

'You want me labelled yellow?'

'No, no, of course I don't, but I don't want you dead, either. If they can't kill you in a straight shoot-out, one of these crazy gunmen will backshoot you and go around boasting they killed the fastest gun.'

'Then somebody would come along and kill him, Wil.'

Anger took a hold on her. She gripped his shoulders and shook him. 'But you wouldn't be here to see it! Can't you see what I'm trying to tell you?'

He could, and he knew she was right, but he was reluctant to admit it. He offered her what passed for a smile. 'Supper smells as if it's about ready. I'll go and wash up.'

As he walked away, her exasperation overwhelmed her love for him and she pushed out something unintelligible that was more of a long drawn out grunt than plain words.

The atmosphere between the three of them was brittle after the supper dishes had been cleared from the table and washed up. It was almost time for Celeste to put little Chloe to bed and she was glad of the chance to be away from the two men for a while. The silence that settled between Winchmore and Jenkins was too much for both of them, but Philip had no intention of leaving him alone with Celeste and Jenkins was aware of the trail his thoughts were taking. The taller man decided he would ride out again and get in some more shooting practice. He had bought more shells from the gunsmith on his way back to the house.

'I'll leave you to enjoy your wife's company,' he said, as he got to his feet. 'Be back around nine.'

Dusk would be settling by then, he reminded himself. He called a farewell to Celeste as he went out to collect his horse.

As he rode out of town he saw Sheriff Kirk Nazeby watching him and, within a half-hour, he knew he was being followed. He found the surveillance amusing. It would not stop him polluting the air with cordite.

When Titus Urquart reported for duty in the morning the sheriff's gaze was sombre.

'He was out target shooting last night, honing up his fast draw, and that means only one thing, Titus.'

'Hardly surprising, Sheriff. He hasn't handled a gun for ten years. which was why he was in the saloon yesterday unarmed. He's got sense enough not to put himself at risk until he's ready to meet the sort of challenge that gunny threw at him yesterday.'

Nazeby shook his head. 'Don't be fooled, Titus. Just because you saved his neck yesterday doesn't mean he won't come gunning for you when he's ready. He wants Wilhelmina back and the only way he can get her is to see you dead.'

'I managed to work that out for myself, Sheriff.'

Nazeby's forehead furrows deepened. 'You don't seem very worried about it.'

'I aim to prove I deserve to keep her.'

'I'll walk down to the store with you, Winchmore.'

The storekeeper had just lifted his hat from the stand. 'Why?'

'I need some shirts and underwear. Might as well give you the business as any o' the other stores in town.'

Walking side by side, Jenkins broke the silence that had developed between them. 'You'll be glad to know I've decided t'let you keep the house, Winchmore. I don't think I could put your wife and little girl out on the street.'

'I'm glad you've been able to see reason, Jenkins. What are your plans?'

'To stay with you for another week or two, till I've finished my business here, then I'll move on.'

Another week or two with little Chloe sleeping

between him and Celeste was not a prospect Winchmore relished, but when he thought of protesting his tongue couldn't get itself around the right words. Maybe he should be thankful that Jenkins was not going to be difficult about the house. Besides, the bank robber had no idea what was in store for him within the timespan involved. Winchmore did not want Celeste getting any more involved with Jenkins than she was already. It worried him that the two of them had spent a lot of time together and there was no knowing just what had gone on between them. His imagination was driving him crazy and he was fearful that Jenkins had already seduced her.

He had to die.

He had left the rifle he bought from Jay Nairn at the store. The caretaker widow woman who now helped out in the store and lived rent free above it was not the sort to ask questions.

Supper was taken almost in silence. Even little Chloe was very quiet for such a small child. Afterwards, Jenkins said he was going out for a while and Winchmore saw his opportunity to go and familiarize himself with that rifle. He told Celeste he was going to get his accounts up to date, having been too busy in the store during the last few days.

He hid the gun under the long duster coat he put on for the purpose and took a long walk out of town. Celeste enjoyed walking and the three of them often took long walks together on the Sabbath. A mile out, he decided that was far enough to avoid attracting attention and he settled himself in a motte of cotton-woods.

He had chosen a Winchester '73 model with the shorter length of barrel, calculating that his marksmanship would not be all that good, even with practice, and he intended to get as close to Duane Jenkins as he could when he killed him. Jay Nairn had shown him how to load the gun when he had expressed idle curiosity and he had memorized the routine well.

The kick from the butt of the rifle against his shoulder came as something of a shock the first time he fired it and the bullet flew far away from the target he had set himself. He was bright enough to realize that he must take a more firm hold on it and aim lower. Thirty shots later he was beginning to acquire more confidence and the prospect of using it for real began to excite him. Killing Duane Jenkins would give him more satisfaction than anything he had ever done in his life.

SEVEN

The hostility from the residents of Eden for which Duane Jenkins had prepared himself had not materialized. While Philip Winchmore had been getting himself accustomed to handling a rifle, Jenkins was reverting to his well-known Mr Nice Guy persona in Bronco Ashurst's saloon, enjoying the talk that his encounter with the crazed gunny the day before had prompted amongst the men. He was now seated with Sheldon King and Dennis Eames.

'You must've been surprised when Titus got you out o' that mess o' trouble,' the saddler said.

'Why would I be surprised, Sheldon? Ain't that what deputy sheriffs are paid for, to protect innocent citizens?'

The saddler was not a man afraid to speak his mind. 'Most folks figured you'd come back t'kill Titus for takin' Wilhelmina off of you.'

Jenkins smiled amiably and there was a twinkle of amusement in his dark eyes. 'Is that what they're sayin'?'

'Sure is.'

'Well I'll be damned. So you figured the deputy would've wanted that drifter t'gun me down, huh?'

'Figures, don't it?'

Jenkins laughed softly. 'Well, I guess you know the man an' I don't, but if Wil wasn't prepared to wait for me, then I reckon he was as entitled as the next man to make a play for her.'

Dennis Eames cut in, 'You mean you don't mind?'

'Sure I mind, but ten years is a long time for a woman t'wait around for a man, ain't it, an' Wil is a beautiful woman. Stands t'reason some man would try t'win her.'

'Must say you seem to be taking it very well,' the dentist acknowledged, 'so why did you head straight back to Eden?'

'I had a home here. Where else would I go?'

'But Wilhelmina sold it while you were in jail, Duane,' King reminded him.

'That's just it, Sheldon. She had no right t'do that. That house is my only asset: a means to start over again.'

Rumour had it that Jenkins had gold stashed away some place, but it was only rumour and King decided not to mention it.

'So you're staying with the Winchmores now,' Eames said casually.

'That's it, at least for a little while. Celeste has been most hospitable.'

'How about Phil?' Sheldon King queried. 'Is he happy about it?'

'Matter of fact, Sheldon, he don't seem to have

49

taken t'me like Celeste an' little Chloe. Why d'you think that is?'

'Aw, come on, Duane, you don't need me t'tell you that.'

They eyed each other through a short spell of cogitation. 'You mean he's scared she might take a shine t'me?'

'Well, you sure had a reputation with women before you went to jail, didn't you?'

'Is that a fact? But then I married Wil, an' that changed me, as you well know.'

'Not what she thinks, Duane. I heard tell it was your womanizin' that persuaded her t'divorce you an' marry Titus Urquart. He don't play around.'

'That don't surprise me. With a face like his he ain't exactly God's gift to women, is he?'

'Seems like your ex-wife decided she preferred kindness an' fidelity to charm, Duane.'

All their heads turned as the batwings opened and Sheriff Kirk Nazeby walked in. He looked around and spotted the three men huddled around the table in the corner and moved towards them.

'Evening, Dennis, Sheldon.'

They returned his greeting while Nazeby fixed his eyes on Jenkins. 'You don't seem very concerned about what happened in here yesterday, Jenkins. Seems to me like you owe us the favour of not inviting more trouble of that nature. I don't want my deputy to have to get you out of that kind of fix again.'

Dark eyes held the sheriff's admonishing stare.

'You mean you want me t'leave town?'

'You were allus bright, Duane, I'll give you that.'

'I've just as much right to stay in Eden as the next man, an' you know it.'

'I'm not talking about rights: I'm talking about you getting yourself or my deputy killed by the next gunslinger who finds out you're here, unless you aim to strap a gunbelt back on, that is, and do your own fighting.'

'Is that what you want?'

'I've told you what I want. You plan to get yourself killed, go some place else and do it.'

Nazeby turned on his heels and went over to talk with Bronco Ashurst.

Jenkins said, 'D'you get the impression he don't like me?'

'That would be the understatement of the year,' Sheldon King told him.

Having never been a heavy drinker, Jenkins knew it would take very little to get him drunk and he had sense enough to remind himself he had been deprived of liquor for ten years. It was, therefore, unwise to linger and he decided to go back to his old home and enjoy watching Philip Winchmore squirm. As he stepped out on to the boardwalk that pleasure was swept from his mind in the instant he recognized the man who faced him.

'Buy you a drink, Duane?'

The man was not nearly as tall as Jenkins, nor was he anything like as personable. There was an ugly

scar slanting diagonally below his left eye and the
toothy grin he flashed at Jenkins had a gap in the
upper jaw.

'No thanks, Zeph, I've had my fill for one night.'

The arrival in Eden of Zeph Minshull sent fingers
of alarm coursing through Jenkins. Nigh on eleven
years is a long time in any man's life and it was always
possible that Minshull was not thinking of the last
time the two men had been together, but if he was,
then what were his intentions?

'You ain't turnin' your back on me again, are you,
Duane?'

'Now why would I do that?'

'Seems like you ain't bein' very sociable.'

'It's been a long day, Zeph. Maybe we could have
that drink tomorrow? You'll still be around, won't
you?'

The grin cane back to Minshull's mouth. 'Oh, you
can count on that, Duane, you can count on that.'

'In that case, I'll meet you here about noon. That
suit you?'

'Don't run out on me, Duane. I wouldn't like that.'

'Now would I do a thing like that?'

'You might. You just might, but we've gotten things
to talk about, Duane. You've been out o' circulation
too long.'

You can say that again, Jenkins mused. He said,
'Goodnight then. Noon tomorrow.'

Duane Jenkins walked away and heard the
batwings swing closed again as his old partner disap-
peared into the saloon. Strapping his gunbelt

around his hips was all right for practice out in the country, but he knew he was not yet ready to do it here in town, with the risk of having to face a challenge. With the arrival of Zeph Minshull he might have to do just that.

EIGHT

Philip Winchmore couldn't believe his luck. He was making his way back to town along the riverbank, the long duster coat again concealing the rifle he had been getting accustomed to handling, and coming towards him was Duane Jenkins, head down, his whole demeanour one of complete contemplation. In a moment of elation, Winchmore noted there was no gunbelt strapped around the outlaw's hips. It was the perfect opportunity. The man he had already begun to hate was defenceless.

Winchmore looked behind him. There was no one else around. He would likely never get a better chance. He ducked behind a cottonwood and drew the rifle from beneath the duster. In his haste to reload it he fumbled and almost dropped the gun, but eventually he levered the first bullet into the breech and stepped out from his hiding place. Jenkins was no more than twenty yards away and the sound of the lever being activated had made him lift his head to see where the danger could be coming from, but when he saw it was Winchmore holding the rifle the surprise, instead of making him take evasive action, brought a grin to his face.

'What in hell are you doin' with that rifle, Winchmore?'

Winchmore levelled the Winchester to aim at the buckle on Jenkins' pants belt.

Jenkins flashed his most disarming smile, but the curl on Winchmore's lips left nothing to the imagination. 'Don't aim that gun at me, man, it might go off.'

Winchmore squeezed the trigger in the instant Jenkins knew for sure the storekeeper intended to kill him.

The bullet struck him in the left side as his feet propelled him sideways in an attempt to get out of the line of fire. As he fell, he heard a second bullet being levered into the breech and he scrambled towards a cottonwood for protection. Winchmore fired again, the bullet hitting Jenkins in the left thigh and, from such close range, passed right through. Yet again the lever was activated and a third shot found a target, hitting Jenkins in the chest and hurling him towards the tree. The victim's body jerked, then lay still.

Looking around him, fearing the shots must have been overheard, Winchmore knew he had to get away before someone came to investigate. He saw no one. Pushing the rifle back under the duster, he hastened up the incline to the trail on the edge of town and forced himself to walk leisurely back to the store.

He let himself in at the back door and stowed the rifle behind the desk in his office.

He needed an alibi, he convinced himself, in case the sheriff remembered how much he had resented the presence of Jenkins in the home he now shared with Celeste. If suspicion should fall on him he wanted a witness to prove he had been in his own store around the time of the shooting. He moved to the foot of the staircase that led to the living-quarters above.

'Quenella!' he called loudly.

The woman opened a door and came to the head of the stairs a few seconds later. 'Yes, Mr Winchmore?'

'I'm leaving now. See you in the morning.'

'Oh. Goodnight then.'

'Goodnight.' He flashed her a smile. 'My wife will be thinking I've run off with another woman.'

She returned his smile. 'I hardly thinks so, Mr Winchmore. You're not that kind of man.'

'I'll take that as a compliment, Quenella. Goodnight again.'

'Goodnight.'

He let himself out of the front door, while she waited for the sound of his key turning in the lock, then she went back to her sitting-room and picked up the book she had been reading.

Shrouded in a fog of pain, the mists of confusion began to clear slowly in Duane Jenkins' mind. Slowly he recalled Winchmore facing him with a rifle and firing shot after shot, then everything had gone black. His body was on fire and his head throbbed.

He lifted his right hand to feel the bump on the side of his head. There was no blood but it felt very tender. He must have hit it on the bole of the tree when he fell, he decided. He tried to rise but pain shafted through him in several places and he lay back to give himself time to get used to the idea that he was seriously wounded.

Trying to get his thoughts into some kind of order, he wondered why no one had come to investigate the shooting. Eden was a quiet town, according to Sheriff Nazeby, and that was how Jenkins remembered it, so gunfire always attracted attention. Then he recalled he had left the town behind him as he walked along the riverbank, trying to decide what to do about Zeph Minshull. The man must have guessed that he would return to Eden when he was released from prison. He would want the pay-off he had been denied when Jenkins had been arrested. Not one to forget a debt, Zeph Minshull.

But now there were more important things to occupy his mind. He must have lost a lot of blood, with wounds in his thigh, side and chest. The weakness that would be the outcome made it imperative that he move and get help. He eased himself into a sitting position and groaned aloud as the pain burned in his chest again.

He sat for a long time before feeling the wounds in his side and thigh. Fortunately the bullets that had caused those wounds had sped right through the flesh. Be thankful for small blessings, he urged himself. If he could get to his feet he would at least be able to walk, even with a bullet hole in his thigh. After he had pushed himself to his feet and stood until everything stopped swirling in front of his eyes, he took his first tentative step forward and promptly fell forward on his face.

As he lay still, waiting once more for nausea to fade away, he was obliged to accept there was no life in his left leg. There was nothing else for it but to crawl. Darkness descended before he had travelled more than a dozen yards. In the distance, a rumble of thunder heralded the coming of a storm.

'Get it all done, did you?' Celeste queried as Philip came into the house.

'Most of it. At least enough to stop me worrying about it. Where's Jenkins?' he asked, feigning ignorance.

'Not back yet. I expect he's found a few old friends to talk with. He's got a lot of catching up to do. So much has happened in Eden since he went away.'

'Since he was jailed, you mean,' her husband sneered.

She raised her eyes sharply at the emphasis he put on the word 'jailed'. 'It's the same thing. Why do you hate him so, Philip? What did he ever do to you before he . . .'

Winchmore's eyes flashed with the hatred she had hinted at. 'Not before, Celeste! Since he came back!'

'What?'

'You know what! He's been making up to you, hasn't he!'

58

She opened her mouth to protest, but he cut in before she could get a word out. 'Don't try to deny it! What's so special about him? You've got me. What do you want another man for?'

'I don't! How could you suggest. . . ?'

He cut in sharply. 'Liar! You think I'm blind? I've seen the way your eyes shine every time you look at him. What's been going on behind my back while I've been at the store?' He pushed himself towards her and grabbed the front of her dress. 'Had your drawers off, has he?'

'Philip! That is an awful thing to say.'

He felt her tremble and her eyes fell, unable to meet his gaze. 'Awful, yes,' he responded, 'but true, isn't it?'

'No!' Even her voice was a squeak instead of a firm denial.

He hit her hard across the face and she fell backwards into the chair she had vacated as she moved towards the door to see if it was Philip or Duane Jenkins returning.

'You slut! Well, tonight, Chloe will sleep in her own bed and you can spread your legs for me.'

'But what about Mr Jenkins?' she asked fearfully.

For answer he turned and locked the door, taking out the key and putting it in his pocket. 'Is the back door locked?'

'Of course. You always insist we keep it locked in the evenings when you're home.'

'Good. Is Chloe in our bed?'

'Of course.'

'Then take her back to her own room. I've been denied long enough.'

She stared at him in perplexity. This was not the man she had married five years ago. Never before had he struck her. She had always submitted meekly to his sexual demands, hating every moment of them, but the thought of him brutalizing her in bed horrified her, especially after the tender loving Duane Jenkins had given her, a glimpse of how exciting and beautiful such union could be.

She turned away in distress, not wanting to antagonize him. As she picked up her daughter she wondered what Duane would do when he came back to the house and found himself locked out. He might become so angry he would kill Philip.

The first few drops of rain spilled onto the street as Sheriff Kirk Nazeby made his way back to his living-quarters at the completion of his final walk round of the evening. Duane Jenkins was probably closeted in the Winchmore home by now, to the intense annoyance of Philip and the possible delight of Celeste. She was not afraid of him and he must have brought a spark of pleasure to her eyes after the dullness of marriage to Philip. Jenkins would have plenty to talk about and Celeste would listen avidly. Nazeby doubted if Winchmore could talk about anything but the store.

'I reckon you'd get more stimulatin' conversation from a dead hound dog,' he recalled Sheldon King saying of Philip Winchmore.

Soaked to the skin, his hat gone and dark wavy brown hair turned almost black with the rain pouring off it, into his eyes and down his neck, Duane Jenkins struggled on, his strength ebbing, the dampness eating into his bones. He was not yet within shouting distance of the nearest dwelling and he wondered how much longer he could crawl in his weakened state. For once in his life he had been mistaken in his assessment of a man. Who would have thought that the one who was known to hate and fear firearms would take up a rifle with the intention of killing one of his fellow humans? Jenkins was convinced that Winchmore thought he had succeeded in killing him when that last shot ploughed into his chest. He would have been in a hurry to get away, afraid of discovery, and he had not bothered to check. Jenkins lying perfectly still, knocked unconscious by his head connecting with the bole of that cottonwood and blood staining his shirt, had no doubt been enough to satisfy Winchmore that he had killed his rival for the affections of Celeste.

Jenkins was almost level with an overhang of rock and decided he needed to gain shelter and rest up awhile before he attempted to crawl any farther. Racked with pain, it took him ten minutes to make cover.

As he waited for his strength to return he wondered what Celeste would do when he failed to return to the house. She was his best, possibly his only hope of help. Without it, would he live to see another dawn?

NINE

Wilhelmina Urquart sensed the tenseness in her husband as she lay by his side. All evening he had seemed like a coiled spring that had been wound too tightly and she knew it was the fear of open conflict between Titus and her former husband that was occupying his thoughts. Not that she felt that Titus was afraid of Duane Jenkins; no, she guessed that he was praying Duane would leave town and let them live together in peace, while at the same time having no faith that the prayer would be answered. Titus was gearing himself up for when the thought of confrontation became a reality. She knew Titus did not want to have to kill Duane, fearing that fact might damage their marriage.

She huddled close to him, feeling the warmth of his body, wanting him to take her in his arms, feel the touch and the passion of his lips on hers, but she knew he would need to be far more relaxed before he could do that. Words of comfort came into her mind, but her tongue could not get around them. She suffered in silence, knowing that was exactly what he was doing. Pride in the knowledge that he would defend her to the last and fight to keep her if there was the slightest danger of Duane trying to take her away from him was her one consolation. She wasn't quite sure that Duane did want her back, but she knew that both her husband and Sheriff Nazeby were convinced of it.

The rain beating against the window panes and on the roof was the only relief from the stifling silence.

Celeste Winchmore cringed as Philip crawled roughly all over her. Never before had he used her so brutally. He seemed intent on hurting her, thrusting into her savagely, determined to make her suffer for the infidelity that she had vehemently denied. This, she accepted, was her punishment for allowing Duane Jenkins to bring a little joy into her almost monotonous life. Hitherto she had only rejoiced in little Chloe, but discovering that the intimacy between a man and a woman could be so exciting had turned her into a liar and an unfaithful wife. In those brief minutes she began to hate her husband.

When he rolled off her, panting from his exertions, she could not escape the wish that it could have been Duane Jenkins lying beside her. He would have wrapped his arms around her and soothed her to sleep, she was quite convinced. Minutes later, Philip was asleep, breathing heavily, and she could still feel the pounding her body had taken from him. As the rain began to beat against the bedroom window she wondered where Duane was.

Where had he got to on such a night?

Why had he not come home?

The minutes dragged by so slowly as she listened for his return and the loud knocking on the door, demanding admittance. As the hours slipped away, she knew that something had happened to him. But what?

He was cold and shivering, weakened by loss of blood and the effort to get back into town and seek help. He knew he must not give in or he would die, but the physical effort needed to follow his instincts was more than his body could summon. His eyelids grew heavy and he slipped into oblivion.

It was still raining heavily when he awoke. His body shuddered and he was shocked into a realization of his position. He could not stay there: he had to move. Half sitting, half lying, he tried to summon the strength to make a move, but there was not enough life left in him to even allow him to sit upright. He called out 'Help!' in a voice he knew was nothing like as loud as his first calls, hours ago, had been.

He wondered what time it was. He had no way of knowing how long he had been asleep. It could have been no more than three or four minutes: it might just as easily have been three or four hours. Why had no one missed him and come searching?

It was still dark. From his position under the rock overhang he could not see the clouds, but he knew that rain was still falling. His wet clothing was stuck to his body, but at least he wasn't getting any wetter. The thought brought him little comfort. He could hardly hope for any kind of help before dawn. Everybody in town would be sound asleep.

He thought of Celeste Winchmore, trying to convince himself that she would be lying awake, wondering what had happened to him. The fact that she could have no inkling it was her own husband, probably snoring beside her, who had shot him, added to the bitter irony of his situation.

What had Winchmore done after he had fled the scene of his crime?

That he would do his best to cover his tracks was not in doubt and, bearing in mind that no one had come looking for Jenkins, it was safe to assume Winchmore had succeeded. Not even Celeste would credit her husband with being capable of trying to murder him. Winchmore hated guns and everyone, including Celeste, was well aware of the fact. Celeste, he decided reluctantly, would assume he had taken a room at the hotel for the night.

Time slid by so slowly he began to fear the dawn was not going to come that day.

The rain had ceased and the rooftops of the town were already steaming under the rising sun as Titus Urquart walked from his modest home to the sheriff's office. Nazeby was seated behind his desk as his deputy came through the door.

'Good morning, Titus. Rough night we had.'

'Ranchers will be thankful, I should think, but they'll tell us we still need a lot more rain.'

'You can bank on it.'

'What's on the cards for today, Sheriff?'

'There's a couple of drunks in back I locked up last night. Reckon we'll fine them ten dollars apiece and turn them loose. Go see if they've sobered up, will you.'

'After that?'

'You want to go collect a few taxes, or would you rather look after the office while I do it? It would give me a chance to have a chat with Celeste Winchmore. See if I can find out what Jenkins is getting up to.'

'I guess it would be better for you to do that, Sheriff. Look a bit too personal if I did it. My guess is Jenkins will ride out of town and get in a bit more shooting practice.'

'Seems like a fair bet. See anything of Philip Winchmore as you walked down here?'

'He was about twenty yards ahead of me. He let himself into the store as I passed by.'

The two drunks grumbled about paying the fines the sheriff demanded, calling ten dollars daylight robbery, but when he said they could either pay up or go in front of the judge in court on a charge of being drunk and disorderly in a public place, disturbing the peace with threatening behaviour, as well as physical assault against each other, they paid and left.

The two officers went through the Wanted posters to refresh their memories, in case any of the outlaws rode into town. They discussed the happenings of the previous evening, with Nazeby mentioning his advice to Duane Jenkins in the saloon and Urquart admitting that there was strain in his home because of the return of Wilhelmina's first husband. The clock had moved around to the hour of nine.

It was just as the sheriff was reaching for his hat to go on his rounds that Celeste Winchmore came into the office in a state of great agitation.

'Hello there, Celeste. What's up?'

'Duane never came home last night. Have you locked him up?'

Both men were struck by the fact that the woman referred to Jenkins by his first name only. 'Duane' was no longer 'Mr' Jenkins.

'Now why would I do that, Celeste?' the sheriff queried. 'Far as I know he hasn't done anything that would warrant me arresting him.'

She looked away from him, deep in thought.

Urquart chipped in. 'He might have taken a room at the hotel, Mrs Winchmore, and forgot to tell you.'

'But all his clean clothes are still at the house.'

'Maybe he'll come back for them today,' Urquart suggested, trying to make her feel better.

The sheriff said, 'Why don't you go ask at the hotel, Celeste?'

The suggestion horrified her and her face showed it. 'Oh, I couldn't do that, Sheriff. Think of the scandal!'

He cottoned to what was going through her mind. 'I'll do it for you, then I'll call at the house and let you know.'

'Oh, thank you, Sheriff. Soon, will it be?'

'I'll make it my first job. You go back to the house

and I'll be with you in about fifteen minutes.'

She thanked him again and went out.

Urquart and Nazeby looked at each other. Nazeby said, 'Looks like Jenkins has cast his spell over Celeste, don't you reckon?'

'I wouldn't know about such things, Sheriff,' Urquart answered with an air of dismissive innocence.

'No. Maybe you wouldn't.' Only Nazeby was not fooled by his deputy's play acting.

He went out and ambled towards the hotel, sensing trouble brewing between Philip Winchmore and his wife. Celeste's concern about Jenkins was far more than idle curiosity.

TEN

He came out of a doze and saw that daylight had come. The rain had ceased, but no one had passed by along the riverbank and seen him. It was a forlorn hope anyway, he recognized immediately. Why would anyone be walking along the footpath at that time of the morning? A few riders exercised their horses this way but most used the wider trails up above, and even if a rider did come by he would sit too high in the saddle to see under the low overhang where Jenkins had sheltered.

His clothes were still wet and when he tried to sit up his wounds stabbed painfully. He felt unbelievably weak, but he knew he had to move to have any hope of assistance.

He felt his thigh wound gingerly. It seemed to have stopped bleeding but felt hot beneath his fingers. Could he possibly get to his feet and walk now? He reasoned that, as his worst fear had not materialized, there was still a chance for survival.

The minutes dragged by while he prepared himself for the effort he knew would be needed. This time he must not make the mistake of making the move until the waves of nausea receded and his mind was cleared of the fog that kept coming and going. The pain of his wounds must not be allowed to hinder his need to get help. He waited patiently, his mind concentrating on Philip Winchmore and what he would do to the man if he survived this totally unexpected turn of events.

He had planned to have his moments of pleasure with Celeste for a week or two, but then he would leave the couple to get on with their lives, once he had disposed of that deputy. Persuading Wilhelmina to leave with him might not be easy, but once she no longer had Titus Urquart to rely on, what option would she have? She had loved him once: he would cast his spell over her again. Not even ten years in prison had robbed him of his power over women. He had already proved that with Celeste Winchmore. Even he was amazed how easily she had surrendered herself to his carnal desires.

Time to make the effort.

He took a deep breath, then let it out slowly after he had crawled out from under the overhang. Another deep breath, then he used his good leg to push himself erect. Gingerly he allowed some of his weight to rest on the other one. The pain shot through him and he gasped sharply.

Ignore it, he told himself. Pain would inevitably be a part of survival. He had to get help and live, if only to riddle Philip Winchmore with bullets. Just take one step at a time: put one foot in front of the other.

He focused his eyes on the backlots of the buildings up ahead and began to walk.

The sheriff soon discovered that Duane Jenkins had not spent the night in the hotel. He made his way to Bronco Ashurst's saloon and discovered that Jenkins had left the saloon shortly after the sheriff had spoken to him the night before. His next call was on the saddler, Sheldon King.

'Missing!' King exclaimed in disbelief. 'Didn't he go back to the house last night?'

'No. Nobody seems to have seen him since he left Bronco's. You any idea where he might've gone?'

'If he didn't go back to the Winchmores', where else would he go?'

Nazeby sighed, summoning all his patience. 'That's what I'm trying to find out, Sheldon.'

'Well, he surely wouldn't up an' leave town at that time o' night. Hell! The man came back to grab Wilhelmina an' I don't see him leavin' without her. Is she. . . ?'

'She was still at home a half-hour ago. Titus is back in the office.'

It was inconceivable that Jenkins had tried to give the impression he had left town last night, then waited to move in on the deputy's wife as soon as Titus had left the house. The possibility had to be investigated though. A law officer's life was full of the unexpected. He left the saddler and hurried to the Urquart home.

He knocked and went straight in. Wilhelmina

71

stared at him in shock, fearing bad news.

'Sheriff! Has something happened to Titus?'

He offered her a disarming smile. 'No, Wil. Titus is just fine. It was you I was worried about.'

'Me? Why?'

'Duane has gone missing.'

She stared hard at him in disbelief. 'Missing! You mean he's left town?'

'We don't know, Wil. I spoke to him about nine last night. It doesn't seem likely that he would have saddled up and ridden out after he left the saloon.'

'Have you checked out at the livery? If his horse. . . .'

'Good thinking. I'd best do that right away.'

'I'll come with you.'

'There's no need.'

'Oh, yes, there is. I want to know if he's gone just as much as you.'

The seven-year-old gelding with the white socks on the front legs that Philip Winchmore had purchased for Jenkins was still in the stall where the outlaw had left him the night before. The livery man had not seen Jenkins that morning but expected him at any time.

'If he shows up, tell him I need to see him urgently,' the sheriff said, 'and make sure you tell him it's only his safety I'm concerned with at the moment.'

'Sure, Sheriff.'

Back out on the street, the deputy's wife put a

hand on Nazeby's arm. 'You think something bad has happened to him?'

His countenance was grave as he looked into her dark-brown eyes. 'I don't know, Wil. I'm plain mystified by the fact he never returned to your old house last night. It didn't make sense that he would leave most of his new clothes and things there and just ride out without a word to anybody. Now we know he didn't, so where can he be?'

He had already told Wilhelmina that it was Celeste Winchmore who had reported him missing. The next line of inquiry stood out in her mind like headlines in a newspaper. 'Let's go talk to her husband, Sheriff.'

'You think he might know something?'

'Doesn't it strike you as odd that *he* didn't come to you and report that Duane had not gone back to the house last night?'

He averted his eyes in contemplation. 'Now you come to mention it, that is a mite odd. He doesn't know that Celeste has done it, either. For her sake, we'd best tread carefully.' He looked back at her. 'Now how about you going into the store and making a few discreet inquiries?'

'Right. I'd best not let him know I'm concerned or that Celeste has been to see you.'

Titus Urquart waited impatiently in the sheriff's office for news of Jenkins, puzzled by the man's disappearance. What was he up to? Had he suddenly decided to forget about his former wife and quit town to start over some place else? Urquart would like to believe that and it occurred to him that the sheriff's first call should have been at the livery stable. If he brought no positive news when he came back, Titus would go in search of Jenkins' newly-acquired horse.

'Good morning, Philip,' Wilhelmina Urquart said, as she faced the storeman across the counter. 'How are you?'

'Good morning, Mrs Urquart. I'm fine. How are you?' She ignored the inquiry about her own health. 'And Celeste?'

'She's fine, too. What can I do for you?'

'Did Duane mention where he was going this morning?'

'Not a word. Why? Do you want to see him?'

'Yes, I do. Maybe he's still at the house. I'll call in on Celeste on my way home.'

Winchmore felt uneasy as he watched her walk out into the street. Maybe he should have told her Jenkins had failed to return to the house last night. The man was dead and it wouldn't be long before someone discovered his body. When she found out, would she suspect him because he had deceived her? And then tell the sheriff?

He began to worry. Maybe he'd best dispose of that rifle.

'That's funny,' Nazeby said, when Wilhelmina told him Winchmore had not mentioned the fact of

Jenkins' failure to return to the house the previous night.

'It might not mean he knows anything, Sheriff.'

'No, but odd, just the same. Why would he pretend Duane had been at the house this morning when we know he wasn't?'

'I don't suppose he likes having Duane staying with them. He was probably relieved when Duane decided to stay out all night.'

He slanted a quick glance at her. 'You mean you think he's been with some woman all night?'

There was a hint of bitterness in her voice as she replied. 'Isn't it the obvious answer? He hasn't bedded a woman for ten years. For a man like Duane, that must have been the hardest part of his years in prison.'

He smiled his relief. 'Now why didn't I think of that? If you hadn't married Titus, I reckon Mr Pinkerton would've been glad to have you on his payroll. You'd make a great detective, Wil.'

'I don't think Mr Pinkerton would share your opinion,' she responded with a dazzling smile.

Deputy Urquart was surprised when his wife preceded the sheriff back into the office, a smile of satisfaction on Nazeby's face.

'Wil! What are you doing here?'

Nazeby answered for her before she could form a reply. 'She's been helping me with my inquiries, Titus, and I think she's solved the mystery.'

'How?'

'We've decided Duane Jenkins is holed up with some woman. We reckon he'll show before the day is much older.'

It was a possibility Urquart had not even considered, but now that he did, he was inclined to agree with them. It seemed like the obvious answer, but he needed to be sure.

'Did you check out the livery for his horse?'

'We did. It's still there, so he can't be far away, though who the woman might be I can't imagine.'

Urquart nodded, then looked at his wife. 'How did you get into this business, Wil?'

'The sheriff wanted to question Philip Winchmore, only he thought that might make him suspicious, if he knew anything about why Duane hadn't gone back to the house last night, so he asked me to make an excuse for wanting to see Duane. Philip never mentioned that Duane hadn't stayed the night in our old home.'

'That's odd. And why didn't Philip Winchmore report that fact to us himself?'

She explained her theory, but a tiny doubt nagged away in his mind. What if Jenkins did *not* reappear, as they expected? Wil's explanation reminded him that Jenkins had made enemies before he had been arrested . . . and some men had long memories.

'Well, let's hope he shows soon, or we might find some jealous husband has harboured a grievance for the last ten years and stuck a knife between his ribs.'

ELEVEN

Her face was distraught when she came to the door in response to the sheriff's knock.

'I'm sorry, Celeste, but it took longer than I figured to check out Duane's movements last night.'

'Have you found him?'

'No, but his horse is still down at the livery and we think he probably spent the night with some woman.' He grinned. 'First thing a man thinks of when he gets out of jail.'

Her eyes flashed anger instead of the relief he might have expected. He knew then for sure that Duane Jenkins had cast his spell on her and the suggestion that he might have bedded another woman was one she hated.

'I expect he'll be back soon, Celeste,' he said.

But he won't get much of a welcome, he added to himself. Whatever had transpired between the outlaw and Celeste Winchmore, it ran deep as far as the woman was concerned. If she had betrayed her husband, maybe the thought of being two-timed herself would help to heal the rift that had probably developed between her and Philip. Jealousy does funny things to people, both men and women.

His progress was slow. but eventually he reached the slope he had walked down last night to get to the path alongside the river. He was almost exhausted and the world swayed before his eyes as he stumbled and fell headlong. Shafts of pain made him cry out, but sheer guts helped him climb the slope on his hands and knees. Once at the top he tried to stand up again. Weakness overcame him and as his vision blurred yet again, he collapsed in a dead faint. He was not aware that the woman hanging out her washing had seen him fall. She rushed over and stared at his bloodstained clothing before she recognized him.

'Duane Jenkins. Looks like somebody tried to kill you. Been womanizing again, have you?'

She turned away and hurried off in search of the sheriff.

Duane Jenkins lay on a soft-covered table in the doctor's surgery as consciousness began to return. He felt a sense of peace that was entirely foreign to him. His body was relaxed and euphoria spread its wings around him.

Content to lie there, wavering between sleep and wakefulness, he slowly became more aware that he was in a strange place. He opened his eyes and saw Sheriff Kirk Nazeby sitting in a chair close by. Shocked into trying to sit up, pain stabbed him in the chest and he fell back again, closing his eyes.

Memory returned.

After a while he opened his eyes again and stared up into the sheriff's face. The lawman had vacated his chair and now stood over him.

'Whoever it was must've been a rotten shot, Jenkins,' Nazeby told him with a grin. 'Who was it?'

No answer.

'Might as well tell me. You'll be in no state to go after him for quite a spell. Let the law take care of it.'

Jenkins' reply was slurred. 'I feel dopey.'

'That'll be the ether Doc Hanson put you to sleep with before he operated. There's one helluva hole in your chest, but you were lucky, I guess. The bullet hit you too high to touch heart or lung. You'll live, the doc reckons.'

Jenkins wondered if Celeste Winchmore had been asking about him.

'Who else knows about it?'

'Reckon half the town by now. You collapsed back of the Inkley house. Martha found you and came running to tell me. Don't reckon it was Nathan who shot you.'

Jenkins remembered he had promised to meet with Zeph Minshull around noon.

'What time is it, Sheriff?'

Nazeby consulted his pocket watch. 'Just after eleven. Why? You got an urgent appointment?'

'Fella by the name o' Zeph Minshull. Promised I'd meet him at Bronco's saloon around noon.'

'Forget it. You're in no state to go any place.'

'He'll think I've run out on him.'

'Well, if it'll make you feel any better, I'll keep the appointment for you. Is he a friend or somebody after your hide?'

'Friend. I owe him.'

'Reckon he'll understand then. You want us to take you back to the Winchmores'? Doc says you can't be moved before sundown, mind. You have to rest or those wounds will start bleeding again.'

Jenkins averted his eyes. 'No.' No sense in giving Winchmore a second chance to finish what he'd failed to do the first time. 'Give me a cot in the jail-house. Reckon I should be safe there.'

'You mean who ever shot you might come after you again?'

He held the sheriff's querying gaze. 'If you thought you'd killed me an' then found out you hadn't, what would you do?'

'I'm no killer, Duane, but I can see what you have in mind.' He thought about it for a moment or two, then asked, 'What about a room in the hotel?'

No matter how much he might hate Nazeby for arresting him and getting him sent to prison for ten years, he knew the sheriff was an honest man. 'I'd be safer with you, 'til I'm on my feet again.'

'I guess maybe you would, at that.' Having Jenkins in constant close proximity would also give Nazeby more time to worm out of him who it was with killing on his mind. 'All right, I'll fix it . . . on one condition.'

'What's that?'

'You forget all about having a showdown with Titus Urquart.'

Jenkins had no intention of doing that, but he needed the protection of the law officer, so he lied, 'Don't reckon I'll be in any state t'brace him after this, Sheriff.'

When news reached Philip Winchmore that he had failed in his attempt to kill Duane Jenkins, fear flooded through him. Would Jenkins have told the sheriff who had shot him? It didn't seem likely, at least for the time being, but then maybe Jenkins had been in no fit state to talk about his ordeal. That situation would not last and Winchmore trembled at the prospect of Sheriff Nazeby coming to lock him up and taking him into court on a charge of attempted murder. It would mean at least five years in prison. Maybe ten. The prospect appalled him.

He had to do something, and quickly. But what?

Kill Jenkins before he recovered sufficiently to talk?

He had the perfect excuse to go and visit Jenkins, bearing in mind the man had been residing with him for the past few days, but he could hardly do that with a rifle under his arm.

Still resting over at Doc Hanson's place, they said. Hanson would understand his interest, but he would be unlikely to leave him alone with the wounded man. Even if he did, Winchmore could not risk killing Jenkins in the doctor's house. Suspicion would immediately fall on him.

But what option did he have? He would be unlikely to get more than one chance.

The first thing would be to find out if Jenkins had talked. If he was not yet well enough there was still a chance of silencing him for good. A knife to the heart was the method that promptly came to mind. Guns were noisy things and he had been fortunate to get back to the store last night undetected. If he could put an end to any threat to himself now, he could always deny any involvement in the death of Jenkins and suggest he had been knifed by an intruder. Even Sheriff Nazeby knew there were husbands still living in Eden whose wives had betrayed them with Jenkins before he had gone to prison. It seemed reasonable that one of them had taken his opportunity to even the score.

Quenella Revett was serving a customer, fully occupied. Winchmore went to the other side of the store and selected a hunting knife, still in its sheath, which he slipped inside his pants. When the customer had paid Quenella and departed, Winchmore turned to her and said, 'Can you cope for a little while, Mrs Revett? I have an errand to run.'

'Of course, Mr Winchmore. Take as long as you like.'

Doc Hanson would still be out on his morning calls, Winchmore reasoned, as he went in back and put on his jacket. Hanson was unmarried and Jenkins was likely alone in the house. As he left the store by the rear exit and came around into the street, Winchmore was fortunate enough to see the medic

ride by in his rig. On his way to a house call, just as
he expected. His luck was still holding, Winchmore
told himself with satisfaction.

He strolled leisurely across the street so as not to
draw attention to himself and made his way by the
back lots to the house where Duane Jenkins was
resting.

'You think you were right, don't you?' Wilhelmina
said, as she poured coffee for her husband to round
off his midday meal. 'It was somebody with a long-
standing grudge against Duane?'

Titus Urquart found little satisfaction in proving
his wife had been wrong about where her first
husband had spent the last night. 'Looks that way to
me. He's barely had enough time to make enemies
since he got back here.'

'The man must have been lying in wait for him.'

'Not necessarily. More likely pure chance
presented itself. How could the would-be killer have
known Jenkins would take a stroll along the riverbank last night?'

'Are you sure it happened last night?'

'The man was soaked to the skin and covered in
mud when he was found, and it hadn't rained since
early morning.'

'And Duane wasn't carrying a gun.'

'I doubt if whoever shot him would have taken the
risk if Duane had been packing a gun.'

With Duane's reputation, that she could believe,

but who could it have been? She searched her memories but failed to come up with a single name.

The rear door of the doctor's house was, surprisingly, unlocked. Winchmore could scarcely believe his luck when the door opened to his quiet turn of the knob. He closed it softly behind him and stood listening. No sound reached his ears. Jenkins would either be in the spare bedroom or still in the surgery.

He moved on cat-soft feet to the bedroom and looked through the open doorway. Taking two steps into the room, he saw that Jenkins was not there. He turned around and made his way towards the surgery, ignoring the small consulting room as he passed by. The door was closed and once again he turned the knob with soft hands, easing it open. He saw Jenkins lying on the operating couch, apparently asleep. Pushing the door wider, he stepped into the room. The knife sheath was now attached to his pants' belt and he withdrew the weapon silently as he moved towards the bed.

'That's close enough, Winchmore!'

He whirled around at the sound of Nathan Inkley's voice. Inkley sat in a chair against the back wall, a shotgun pointing straight at Winchmore's belly.

TWELVE

'Drop the knife!'

Winchmore began to shake all over but his hand still clutched the knife.

'Drop it or I'll blast you t'hell!'

The command roused Duane Jenkins from his slumber and as soon as he opened his eyes he saw Philip Winchmore standing there, shaking like a leaf. 'You!'

'So it was him who shot you, Jenkins.' In Inkley's mind the time for conjecture was over.

The wounded man eased himself onto his left elbow. 'What makes you think that?'

Winchmore panicked, dropped the knife and ran from the room, hurling himself towards the back door of the house. He wrenched it open and fled, not bothering to waste time closing it again.

He hurried back to the store, knowing his secret was out. Now Nathan Inkley would be a witness against him. Inkley would testify that he had raised a hunting knife to strike Jenkins as he lay asleep in the doctor's surgery. It was no longer just his word against that of Jenkins. Prison bars loomed large in

Winchmore's mind's eye. He had to get away.

Entering the store by the rear entrance, he went through and emptied the till of every cent, to the consternation of Quenella Revett. 'Aren't you going to leave me any change, Mr Winchmore?'

He ignored her and raced to his office. He unlocked the safe and stuffed notes and coinage into his pockets, then raced outside again and ran towards the bank. He had only one hope of getting more money and leaving town before the sheriff was alerted. If the sheriff had thought it necessary to leave Nathan Inkley to guard Duane Jenkins, then Inkley would not dare to leave him.

The bank president was astounded when Winchmore said he wanted to withdraw $10,000.

'Whyever do you need so much all at once, Philip?'

'Never mind why! Just get it for me. Now! It's my money and I want it.'

The bank president sighed heavily. 'All right, Philip, if that's what you want.'

He fingered his keys and moved towards the safe.

'I'll be back in five minutes. Have it ready for me.'

'It will take me more than. . . .'

He never finished the protest as Winchmore fled the office.

Winchmore hurried to the livery stables and saddled his horse. The liveryman was caught on the hop, seeing the storekeeper at that time of the day. 'Going some place, Mr Winchmore?'

There was no reply and the liveryman knew better

86

than to pursue the matter.

Horse saddled and bridled, Winchmore led him outside and mounted, heading back to the bank.

Money was laid out on the president's desk, waiting to be checked. 'Put it in a bag, quickly!'

'Don't you want to check it?'

'I trust you. Get a bag!'

It took no more than a minute to stuff the bills, of various denominations, into a bag. Winchmore grabbed it and raced from the office, back to his horse. He decided he would like that rifle with him in case he should need it to protect himself. It would only take him a couple of minutes to get the gun and the few remaining shells he had not used in practice. When he entered the store from the rear again he was glad to note that his assistant was busy with a customer. As he went to his office he wondered if she had even noticed his return. He collected the rifle and was gone and mounted again before the customer had been satisfied.

He headed out into the street and raced north, followed by the astonished stares of some townsfolk, who seldom saw Winchmore out riding, and certainly not in the middle of the day.

Where could he be going in such an all-fired hurry, they asked themselves? Sheriff Kirk Nazeby was one of then, but he had an appointment to keep and that was uppermost in his mind.

'You happen to be Zeph Minshull?' the sheriff asked the stranger who sat at a table in Bronco Ashurst's saloon, a bottle and glass in front of him. Nazeby noticed the scar on his left cheek.

'Didn't know I was that famous, Sheriff. Don't tell me I've broken the law here in Eden!'

'Not as far as I know.'

The sheriff sat down opposite Minshull, struck by the mop of unruly dark hair above a lined forehead and keen brown eyes. He was wearing a blue shirt, frayed at the collar, and looked as if he might not have two cents to rub together.

'Then what can I do for you, Sheriff?'

'You expecting Duane Jenkins to meet you here about now?'

'Matter of fact. . . . Don't tell me that bastard ran out on me again! I'll kill him!'

'No, he didn't run out on you. He fully intended to meet with you, only somebody used him for target practice last night.'

Minshull's eyes widened. 'He's dead?'

'No, but he was badly wounded and it'll need some time for him to get fit again. I can take you to see him, if you like?'

'Sure, Sheriff, I would like that.'

'He said you were a friend, only I have a problem with that. You didn't sound much like a friend just now.'

Full lips extended into a half smile. 'Just my little joke, Sheriff.'

'Killing in Eden is no joke, Minshull. You lay a finger on Jenkins and you'll end up in jail, pronto!'

Minshull spread his hands as his shoulders lifted.

'Like Duane told you, we're friends.'

'You'd better be. Come on then, let's go visiting.'

As soon as the two men entered the house, Nathan Inkley moved into the hallway, shotgun held ready for action at his waist. 'Oh, it's you, Sheriff.'

Concern had been written all over Inkley's face in the moment he appeared. Nazeby asked, 'What's wrong, Nathan?'

'Philip Winchmore, that's what's wrong.'

'Winchmore? What's he got t'do with this business?'

'He snuck in, quiet as a mouse, intendin' t'finish off what he started last night.'

The sheriff couldn't believe what he was hearing and his voice betrayed his incredulity. 'Winchmore?'

'He had a huntin' knife in his hand, ready to finish off Jenkins.'

'Well I'll be damned. So he's made his getaway.'

'What you mean, Sheriff?'

'He rode out of town like a bat out of hell, about ten minutes ago. Is Jenkins all right?'

'He's fine, Sheriff.'

'I've brought him a visitor.'

Nazeby led the way into the surgery and glared at Jenkins, 'Now why the hell didn't you tell me it was Winchmore who shot you last night?'

'Would you've believed me?'

The small silence was all the answer Jenkins needed. 'I thought not. Winchmore hates guns an' everybody knows it, includin' you. You'd've thought

89

I was prevaricatin', wouldn't you?'

'I guess I would.' The sheriff would have sworn there was no gunbelt around Winchmore's hips as he rode out of town, but there might have been a rifle pouched on the blind side. 'What gun did he use last night?'

'A Winchester rifle. I guess that's why the bullets went straight through my leg an' side. An' now you've spoiled my plan t'teach that dumbcluck a lesson.'

'Not me, Duane. Winchmore did that himself. I guess I'd best get after him, but not before I've eaten. Should be able to pick up his trail easy enough.' He turned to look at Zeph Minshull. 'I brought you a visitor. You sure it's safe to leave him here with you?'

In spite of the ache in his body, Jenkins managed to summon a grin. 'Howdy, Zeph.'

'You want I should go after this guy with the sheriff?'

'I don't reckon that'll be necessary. Sheriff Nazeby is good at his job. He'll bring Winchmore back for trial.'

The threat to Jenkins' life seemed to have evaporated, so the sheriff told Nathan Inkley to go get himself some lunch. 'Looks like you won't be needed for a while, Nate.'

'I am a mite peckish, an' that's a fact.'

'I'll leave a message for my deputy, Duane. See you when I get back.'

Nazeby and Inkley departed together and Minshull took the vacant chair.

'What brought you to Eden, Zeph?'

'I'm flat busted, Duane. Heard you were due for release and figured you'd head back t'that pretty wife o' yours.'

Jenkins saw no point in acquainting Minshull with the fact that Wilhelmina was now somebody else's wife, at least not for the moment.

'You also figure I'd have a plan worked out t'relieve some bank president of his assets?'

'I guess that's about the size of it. You ran out on me last time an' you owe me, Duane.'

'I didn't run out on you, Zeph; it was you who ran out on me. I'm the one who got arrested an' I'm the one who's just done ten years in that stinking prison. I reckon that puts a different complexion on the situation.'

It was a point Minshull was reluctant to concede. 'What about the money?'

'Far as I know it's still where I left it.'

'Only you ain't in no fit state t'ride an' get it.'

'I can let you have enough to tide you over, if you come back later.'

'How much later?'

'After supper. They plan t'move me t'the jailhouse around sundown. Doc reckons I have t'rest until then.'

'Jailhouse? You under arrest again?'

'No, Zeph. We just agreed I'd be safer there, in case that Winchmore had another go, once he found out I was still alive.'

'I see. Where can I put on a feedbag on credit, Duane?'

'Can you see my pants anywhere?'

Minshull stood up and looked around. There was no sign of any bloodstained clothing. 'Reckon the medic has gotten rid of 'em. Were they all messed up?'

'I guess they were.' The two made eye contact again. 'Why don't you go to the eating-house down the street,' Jenkins suggested. 'Ask Velda to feed you an' put it on my slate. Tell her to send me something to eat while you're at it. She knows I'll settle with her when I get the chance.'

'You want I should go now?'

'Sure. Seems like there's no threat t'me now, an' I'm hungry, tell Velda.'

Titus Urquart got back to the office just as the sheriff was saddling his dappled grey. 'I've left you a note on my desk, Titus. It was Philip Winchmore who shot Jenkins. He's skipped town. I'm going after him.' He settled his Winchester rifle in the saddle pouch and climbed into the saddle. 'You do those errands I've left you and keep an eye on a fella by the name of Zeph Minshull. Seems he's an old pard of Jenkins.'

The sheriff kicked the grey into a fast gallop. Urquart watched him go, then went inside to read his instructions.

He left the office, locking the door behind him, remounted his dun mare, and headed for the Winchmore home. Celeste's face was not exactly welcoming when she opened the door.

'Hello, Mrs Winchmore. How are you?'

92

'I'm all right. What brings you here, Deputy Urquart?'

'Sheriff asked me to come and see you. Have you heard about Duane Jenkins?'

'What about him?'

'The sheriff had it all wrong when he spoke with you this morning. Jenkins was shot last night.'

Her face showed animation for the first time. The surprise and concern in her eyes for Jenkins told him she was unaware that her husband had gone on the run.

'Shot!?'

He allowed her a couple of heartbeats to take in the news before asking, 'Can I come in?'

She stood aside, opening the door wider to admit him. 'Go through.'

She followed after she closed the door. 'Is he dead?'

'No, the doc thinks he'll live, but he was shot three times. Worst was a bullet in the chest, but high up. Missed both heart and lung.'

He sensed her relief as she let out a small sigh, then invited him to sit. She took the chair opposite. 'Who did it?'

'You really don't know?'

'Of course not. How could I?'

'It was your husband, Mrs Winchmore.'

'Philip? I don't believe it!'

'He's done a bunk. The sheriff has gone after him. He'll be charged with attempted murder.'

'But Philip hates guns. He's afraid of them.

93

Everybody knows that.'

'Well it seems he got over that fear.' Urquart figured he knew why. 'Did you give him cause to be jealous of Jenkins?'

Colour stained her cheeks. 'Whatever makes you think that?'

'It's the obvious explanation, Mrs Winchmore. Why else would Philip try to kill Duane Jenkins?'

She could see there was no point in denying it, but she still had to come to terms with the idea of Philip taking up a gun to kill even Duane. 'I suppose Phil was a bit jealous of Duane.' A strange laugh gurgled in her throat. 'He has this reputation with women, don't you know.'

'Yes, I know.'

The silence stretched, until he said, 'Anything I can do for you, Mrs Winchmore?'

'No. No, thank you.'

He got to his feet. 'Maybe you'd best go and see Quenella Revett and tell her what's happened. Better for her to hear it from you than me.'

'Yes, I suppose so. I'll have to take Chloe with me. She's out back, playing.'

'I'm really sorry, Mrs Winchmore.'

She nodded in silence. He headed for the door, wondering what the future held for Philip Winchmore's wife and daughter.

As he remounted the mare a consoling thought came to him. He could stop fretting about Duane Jenkins bracing him on the streets of Eden, at least for a week or two. He'd best go and see him, then maybe he would get a better idea of how long a reprieve he had.

THIRTEEN

Sheriff Kirk Nazeby rode at a steady lope, conserving his mount's energy in case Winchmore eluded him for more than a day, which Nazeby thought unlikely. The fugitive was unaccustomed to long rides and, apart from his business acumen as far as the store was concerned, not very bright. Having ridden out of town in a hurry, he had probably run his chocolate and white pinto into the ground before being obliged to give him a breather. Nazeby thought it unlikely the man had even considered taking food with him; maybe not even a water bottle. His actions would have been that of a man panicked by discovery, knowing that time was not on his side once his actions at the doctor's house became known, counting on putting distance between hinself and a posse he would expect to chase after him.

The gelding would stand out against any background, with all that white on him, and the sheriff was well versed in the art of manhunting. Winchmore would need to find good cover to avoid being spotted. Nazeby was confident of catching up with him before sundown. That pinto spent too much time in the stables to have built up the stamina needed for a long run.

Doctor Tod Hanson looked in on Duane Jenkins as soon as he returned from his calls, glad to see his patient had fully recovered from the effects of the anaesthetic.

He offered Jenkins a smile. 'How are you feeling now?'

'Sore, Doc.'

'That's a bad chest wound, but the others should heal quite well in a week or two. Don't try to rush your recovery.'

'How long, Doc?'

'A month, at least, providing we can keep the chest wound free from infection. I'll need to examine you twice a day, just to make sure everything is taking a normal course.'

'You mean I'll have t'sit around an' do nothin' for a whole month?' The prospect appalled Jenkins.

'If you want to live. A small price to pay, I'd say. You concentrate on how you're going to pay my bill, which won't be small, taking into consideration all the attention you'll need.'

Jenkins didn't need to worry about that, now that Wilhelmina had handed over the money from the sale of the house. With the interest it had accrued over a five-year period it had grown into a handy amount.

97

'That reminds me, Doc, what happened to my moncy belt?'

'It's safe. Whoever shot you did not have robbery on his mind.'

That he didn't, Jenkins told himself, but it was of little consolation.

'Could you bring me the belt? I'll give you a down payment. Another thing, I've sent a friend o' mine to get Velda at the eating-house to send me somethin' to eat. Should be here any minute. I'm hungry, Doc.'

'That's a good sign. I'll get your belt.'

It was at this juncture that Titus Urquart arrived. Jenkins was wary of him and it showed in the stare he fixed on the deputy.

'How is he, Doctor?' Urquart asked.

'He should be well enough to move this evening, but when you do take him down to the jailhouse, make sure he has a slow, easy trip. I've gotten a stretcher you can use to carry him. If you'll excuse me a moment, Deputy?'

'Sure, Doc.' Urquart fixed his eyes on the wounded man. 'They tell me you're lucky to be alive.'

'I won't argue with that. Three tries at killin' me an' that bastard couldn't even get one where it counted.'

'And you without a gun to defend yourself. Now that surprises me. How come a man with your reputation was wandering around like a toothless cougar?'

'Without a gun I couldn't be drawn into a shoot-out, could I?'

'Been out practising though, haven't you.' Urquart made it a statement, not a question.

'You been keepin' tabs on me?'

'Sheriff, more than me. He worries about you.'

He's a damn sight more worried about you than me, Jenkins was reminded, but he kept the thought to himself.

'Well, right now he's gotten somethin' more important t'worry about. That Winchmore will shoot Nazeby just like he shot me if the sheriff ever catches up with him.'

'But you and me both know Winchmore is a rotten shot, and so does the sheriff.'

Jenkins could not resist the urge to put a damper on the deputy's complacency. 'Winchmore has to get lucky some time.'

In the afternoon Celeste Winchmore could no longer resist the need she felt to see her lover. She decided that if anyone criticized her for such action, she would tell them she felt the need to apologize for what her husband had done. She left Chloe with a neighbour and made her way to the doctor's house.

The doctor stared hard at her as she stood at the door. 'Why, Mrs Winchmore!'

'How is he, Doctor?'

'He'll live, hopefully.'

'Can I see him?'

'Do you think that's wise?'

'It's all my fault, Doctor. I need to apologize.'

Hanson debated with himself for only a moment,

recalling that his patient had been staying with Celeste and Philip. 'All right, if that's what you want. Come in.'

He closed the door as she stood just inside the hallway. 'But first I must ask my patient if he is willing to receive you. In view of the fact that it was your husband who shot him, as I understand, he may not welcome you.'

'In that case. . . .'

He gave her an encouraging smile. 'I won't be a moment.'

Jenkins agreed to the visit and the doctor left the two of them alone to chat.

'I'm sorry, Duane, I really am. It's all my fault.'

'Oh, no, you can't blame yourself. Let's face it, Celeste, I took advantage of you.'

'That's the one good thing about this whole business. I wanted you just as much as you wanted me. You gave me something I'd never had before.'

He didn't need to ask what she meant.

'Could you get my stuff down to the jailhouse for me? The doc has incinerated the clothes I was wearing.'

'I'll ask Deputy Urquart to collect them for you.'

'That would be best, I guess. You've gotten little Chloe to worry about now. You can say goodbye t'that husband o' yours. He'll either end up dead or in jail after what he's done.'

'I know.' She hesitated, wondering if she dare to voice the wish that was going through her mind. Her decision made, she said, 'Why don't you get them to bring you back to your old home? I could nurse you until you're fit and strong again.'

It was a much better idea than spending his days and nights on a cell cot, but what would the townsfolk say?

'I'd like that a lot, Celeste, only I ain't so sure it's a good idea. Don't reckon the sheriff would go for it.'

'What can he do for you that I can't?'

Ignoring the aches and pains of his flesh, he flashed her his most seductive smile. 'Not a damn thing.'

He was walking the dappled grey now, watching for signs that Winchmore might have turned off the trail and hidden himself in the hills. His pinto would be weary and once he headed into the canyon up ahead there was no way but forward, with fewer places to hide. Maybe that was something Winchmore had not taken into consideration, but the sheriff knew the terrain far better than the man he was chasing.

A half-hour later the sheriff knew Winchmore had got himself in a no-return situation. The canyon walls were high and in places the floor was narrow. In the wider sections there were large boulders to shield a man and Nazeby remained watchful.

He slowed his horse and, minutes later, heard a whinny up ahead. He brought the grey to a halt and scanned the rocks a hundred yards in front and away to his left. Winchmore was not far away, probably hunkered down some place feeling sorry for himself and watching his backtrail. He likely knew exactly where the sheriff was at that moment, out in the open, an easy target for a man trained in the use of firearms, but at that distance Winchmore couldn't hit a barn door, Nazeby assured himself.

He steered the grey away to his left, got down from the saddle and picketed him. Withdrawing his Winchester from the saddle pouch, the sheriff scampered to the other side of the canyon on foot. If he could draw Winchmore's fire he would have a better idea where he was hiding. The pinto would not be so easy to conceal.

He called out in a voice that echoed loudly in the confined space. 'Come on out, Winchmore! Give yourself up! You're trapped and there's no way out.'

For an answer Winchmore triggered his rifle, the bullet hitting the rockface a dozen yards away to Nazeby's right. The sheriff did not see the flash of flame that came from the gun but he was well able to judge Winchmore's position by sound alone.

'Go back, Sheriff! I don't want to kill you, but I will if you make me.'

'I'll go back when you're ready to come back with me. Don't be a fool, Philip.'

'I won't go to jail. It would kill me.'

'You'd be out in five years, maybe less. I'm taking you back, dead or alive.'

Another bullet hit the canyon side and whined away harmlessly.

'You're not very good with that thing, Winchmore.'

'But I'm getting better,' Winchmore yelled back.

'Next time I'll kill you. Go back and leave me alone.'

The sheriff knew within a few yards just where Winchmore was hiding, but he could not see him. The pinto was now within his vision, but the fugitive might have left it there as a decoy. His voice had been coming from a distance away.

'Come on out, Philip, or I'll shoot the pinto. You'll get nowhere without it.'

There was a short silence before Winchmore responded. 'You wouldn't do that, Sheriff. You love horses too much.'

Smart enough to know my weaknesses, Nazeby acknowledged ruefully, but he could not allow Winchmore to score points off him. 'But I hate killers more and that's what you nearly became, Philip. Think yourself lucky. You could be on a hanging charge. You only wounded Jenkins, so give yourself up.'

'No!'

'I know where you are. I'm coming in.'

He moved along the canyon side in short bursts, zig-zagging in case Winchmore loosed off a lucky shot. He heard boots scraping on rock and knew Winchmore was moving. Moments later they faced each across the floor of the canyon. Winchmore lifted his rifle and fired. The bullet tore into Nazeby's left arm above the elbow and exited, leaving a hole in the shirt and flesh that threw the sheriff off balance. He levelled his own rifle with his one good arm and squeezed the trigger. He saw Winchmore hurled back by the force of the bullet hitting him in the chest, his own gun falling.

The sheriff moved forward as Winchmore clutched at his chest, then collapsed to his knees. Nazeby was not sure if it was the damage his bullet had done or the shock of being hit that made the fugitive crumble. Shock is a powerful thing for any man to have to accept the first time he gets shot.

Winchmore looked up at Nazeby as he came close. 'You shot me!' he exclaimed in wonder, his voice little more than a whisper.

'You shot me first, Philip.' The sheriff knew his own wound was by far the less serious of the two. 'Let's call a truce. I'll attend to your wound if you see to mine.'

FOURTEEN

The sheriff lowered his rifle and laid it on the ground. When he looked at Philip Winchmore again he saw the eyelids had shuttered. Whether it was the result of his own wound or the sight of blood on Nazeby's sleeve the sheriff could only surmise. Ignoring the pain and the blood running down his arm and over his left hand, Nazeby opened the buttons on Winchmore's shirt. The bullet had made a neat hole in his chest, to the left of his heart and Nazeby knew it was life-threatening. If it had punctured Winchmore's lung, his time was fast running out.

Nazeby had a struggle to remove Winchmore's coat with only one good hand, but when it came to the shirt he was less gentle, ripping it while the wounded man remained unconscious. The sheriff hauled him forward and looked over Winchmore's shoulder for an exit wound. There was none. He could see something dark on the surface of the skin, indicating that the tip of the bullet seemed to be close to Winchmore's spine and Nazeby knew that was bad, cutting the odds of survival. As he laid him down again Winchmore coughed heavily and blood oozed from his mouth. No way was he going to be able to ride back to Eden.

The sheriff searched Winchmore's pockets for something with which to plug the wound. He found a clean white handkerchief and began to press it into the hole the bullet had made, not sure if he was making the right decision. Winchmore went into another spasm of coughing and yet more blood poured from his mouth. His body sagged and Nazeby was not quick enough, hampered by his own wound, in turning Winchmore over on his side. The store-keeper choked on his own blood. His body shuddered, then lay still.

The sheriff sighed with regret. Winchmore's jealousy of Duane Jenkins had brought about his death. What a waste. Having to go and inform Celeste that she was not only a widow, but that it was his bullet that had killed Philip, was a prospect which made Nazeby more depressed than he could have imagined.

With the hundred dollars in his pocket that Duane Jenkins had given him early that afternoon, Zeph Minshull sat in the saloon pondering his options. Jenkins had offered him another thousand dollars to pick a fight with Deputy Urquart and kill him, paving the way for Duane to reclaim his wife. No blame could be laid at Jenkins' feet if the deputy was killed by another man's gun. Minshull could see his old pard's reasoning and he did have confidence in his own ability to outdraw any man, other than Duane Jenkins himself. He might even be faster than Jenkins now, taking into account that his old buddy had been out of circulation for ten years. That was why Duane had put the proposition to him. Briefly, Minshull had considered taking the hundred dollars and riding out, but then he thought of his share of the money the two men had taken from the last bank robbery they committed together and that made up his mind for him. His share, plus a thousand dollars for killing Urquart, was too much to pass up, even if it did mean waiting until Duane was fit to ride again. The problem was how to get Deputy Urquart sufficiently riled to go for his gun. Better to get it done while the sheriff was away on the trail of the man who had tried to kill Duane.

He sat for an hour, hoping Urquart would come into the saloon, giving him a chance to pick a quarrel with the deputy, but Urquart never showed.

Minshull went to look for him.

Recognizing that obeying doctor's orders was his best chance of recovery, Duane Jenkins knew it would be some time before he could hump Celeste again and, therefore, he settled for the discomfort of the jailhouse rather than the warmth of the bed the woman would have made for him. He would be bored out of his mind, but then he'd had plenty of practice in the art of letting time pass by while he was in prison, so if he was able to get Wilhelmina back at the end of his recuperation it would be worth it.

Supper was the only thing he had to look forward to after Celeste departed, apart fron the possibility of news that Zeph had managed to get rid of the deputy sheriff. In that event, with the sheriff out of town, he reckoned Doc Hanson would put up with him for another night.

Celeste Winchmore was not unduly concerned about having to cope with life without a husband. It would only be for some years if the sheriff brought him back to stand trial, but even if Philip got clean away, he would never dare to return. The store would be hers and, with Quenella Revett to help her run it, her livelihood was still assured. As a butcher's daughter she knew a little about profit and loss and she could learn all she needed to know with Quenella to assist her. Her biggest fear was that Duane Jenkins would ride off and leave her, once he was fit again. She sighed mournfully as she prepared supper for herself and Chloe.

Where is Philip now? she asked herself.

Has the sheriff caught up with him yet?

The deputy's wife was wondering if her husband was on his way home as her cooking reached an advanced stage. It was ready to serve and if he was late it would spoil.

She had contemplated visiting Duane earlier, just for the hell of it. Seeing him lying still, nursing bullet wounds, would have given her the perverse pleasure of telling him it had been bound to happen one day.

He couldn't keep on seducing other men's wives without one of them going gun-crazy some day.

Titus Urquart came through the door and she forgot all about Duane Jenkins. Her welcoming smile gladdened the deputy's heart.

'I have to go back on the streets again, Wil. Sheriff might not get back tonight. Can't leave the town with no law all night.'

'Maybe I'll go and see Celeste, see if I can cheer her up. She must be feeling awful by now.'

'You do that. It would be a kindness.'

He reached for his hat, then strapped his gunbelt around his hips.

'You take care now, Titus,' she said, putting her arms around his neck and giving him a fond kiss. 'I need you.'

The sheriff walked the horses back towards town, Winchmore's body slung over the pinto's back. Nazeby was hungry: his wound aching. He cursed the dead man out loud It would be midnight before he got back to Eden and Velda's eating-house would be closed.

At least Doc Tod Hanson would not grumble at being roused from his bed to treat the wounded arm and pronounce Philip Winchmore dead.

Zeph Minshull's patience began to wear thin. He had seen the deputy on the street through the window of the eating-house as he sat eating his supper, but the food was more enticing at that hour. There would be time later to dispose of Urquart.

But, since that time, he had failed to catch a glimpse of the deputy. Exasperated, he went back to the doctor's house to have a few more words with Jenkins.

After the doctor had been called out to attend the birth of a baby, Minshull again brought up the subject of getting rid of Titus Urquart.

'Where the hell does he get to, Duane?'

'With the sheriff out o' town, he'll have plenty t'do. This is a big town, Zeph. Anyhow, you might be wise to backshoot him after dark. Like I told you this afternoon, he's real fast.'

'I ain't never gone in for backshootin', Duane.'

'You ain't never come up against a man as fast as Urquart before, either. Believe me, I've seen him. Wait 'til after dark. He'll be down at the depot to meet the night train around ten o'clock. Ain't usually many folks around at that time. Should be your best chance t'get him alone, when he leaves t'go back to the sheriff's office. No witnesses means nobody gets arrested.'

'Mebbe you're right, but I'll call him out before I shoot. A bullet in the back invites a murder charge.' He fingered his neck. 'Don't take t'the idea of a rope necktie.'

'Then just make sure you get the first shot in. A thousand dollars is no good to a dead man.'

The change from sundown, through dusk to darkness, was but a short time. Titus Urquart's mind was with Sheriff Nazeby, wondering if he had caught up with the fugitive and, if he had, what had transpired between them, more than on what he was doing, checking the business premises and the bank to make sure they were all locked up for another night. Satisfied, he made his way down to the depot to await the coming of the night train. There was no one else around that he could see and he went along to the depot office to have a word with the telegrapher. They talked at length about the shooting of Duane Jenkins and the departure of Philip Winchmore before they heard the whistle blow down the track, announcing the approach of the train.

A mail sack was dropped off, seven passengers alighted and hastened to their homes; none climbed aboard. Urquart watched the train depart until it was lost in the darkness, then he turned and began to walk back into town.

It was then he heard someone call his name.

FIFTEEN

In the darkness Urquart did not see the gun in Zeph Minshull's right fist. Instinctively, at that time of night and realizing that someone was behind him, his own hand flew to his Smith & Wesson .44, but even as he whirled and saw the pale shadow of a man's face, the first bullet ripped into him, hurling him backwards. The second slug struck him high in the shoulder as he tried to raise his own gun to fire back. He fell sideways and lay still.

Minshull moved towards him, intent on making sure the deputy was really dead. As he stooped to bend over him, Urquart opened his eyes and squeezed the trigger once, then life slipped away from him.

Caught like a sucker, Minshull stumbled backwards, cursing as the bullet thudded into him from close range. He toppled to the ground, his gun falling from his grasp. Feeling his shoulder where the bullet had entered, he was relieved to find it had sped right through, entering at an angle just below his collarbone and exiting through the fleshy part, but the burning pain was worse than anything he had ever known.

The long silence was eventually broken by running feet. He crawled away no more than half a dozen yards before the telegrapher arrived to find out what had started all the shooting. Shortly afterwards two more men came on the scene.

'What was all the gunplay, Stavros?'

'Deputy Urquart. He's been shot. Looks like he's dead. We wuz talkin' t'gether just a while back. There's another feller over there.'

'He shot me,' Zeph Minshull said, climbing painfully to his feet. 'I need that sawbones.'

All three men stared at him and, even in the dark, they could see he was not holding a gun and his holster was empty. One of them stepped towards him and trod on a revolver. He stooped and picked it up.

He looked up at Minshull. 'This yours?'

'I guess so. I dropped it.'

'Before he shot you or after?'

Minshull was no fool. He recognized the question as a trap. He recalled he had fired twice as against the deputy's once. 'After I'd fired back. No lawman should shoot an innocent man like that,' he protested in an aggrieved tone. 'I only wanted to ask him if the sheriff had gotten back to town.'

The telegrapher said, 'You'd best get that wound seen to. You know where the doc's house is?'

'Sure. I was there visitin' this afternoon.' He looked at the man who was holding his gun. 'Stick that back in my holster, will you?'

113

'No. This gun killed the deputy. It'll have to be handed over to the sheriff. He'll want to conduct an investigation. He ain't gonna be exactly jumping for joy when he finds out you've killed his deputy.'

Minshull glared back. 'It was self-defence!'

'Then you've nothing to worry about.'

Without his weapon, Minshull was in no position to argue. 'In that case I'll go see the doc an' get this wound fixed.'

'You do that. You staying at the hotel?'

'For t'night, at least.'

'I'll tell the sheriff.'

Minshull turned away and they watched him until the darkness swallowed him.

The telegrapher said to the one holding Minshull's gun, 'I'll have to go back and lock up the depot office, Farley. Reckon you two had best take the deputy to the sheriff's office. Expect you'll find the keys in his coat pocket.'

'Sure, we'll do that. Hope that sheriff gets back soon.' Farley Arkwright pushed the gun into his pants' belt and bent over. 'I'll take his shoulders, Busby, if you'll grab his legs.'

They lifted the dead deputy and carried him the 200 yards to the sheriff's office, lowered him to the boards under the stoop and searched his pockets to find the door key.

'You got a match, Farley? We need a light to sort out which key opens this door.'

A lantern was turned down low in the office and,

once inside, they carried the deputy to a cell and laid him on the cot. Their arrival awakened Duane Jenkins, who had only just fallen asleep. The two men had earlier watched the deputy and Nathan Inkley stretcher Jenkins to the jailhouse and so they were not surprised when he pushed himself gingerly up on one elbow.

'Who you got there?' he asked in the gloom.

'Deputy Urquart. He's been shot by that feller who arrived in town last night.'

'Zeph Minshull?'

'Yeah,' Farley Arkwright answered. 'Friend of yours, ain't he?'

Jenkins feigned ignorance. 'How'd it happen?'

'We don't know. We weren't there. All we heard were the shots, but I reckon that Minshull will have some explaining to do when Sheriff Nazeby gets back. If he don't skip town first, that is.'

'Where is he now?'

'Gone to see Doc Hanson,' Busby Gawber told him. 'The deputy don't miss when he aims his gun at a man.' Then he realized what he'd said. 'Leastways, he didn't.'

Minshull must have fired before the deputy could get his gun drawn and aimed, Jenkins decided, just like I advised him. And not a soul to prove it was anything but self-defence. Zeph would not run. He would stick around and even risk the outcome of a trial, if it came to that. Pleading self-defence when there was no one to argue made the odds on an acquittal very good indeed. No, Zeph would not

115

run. He would be too interested in that thousand dollars, as well as wanting his share of the buried loot.

Wilhelmina Urquart looked at the clock again, as she had done at least a dozen times in the last hour. Titus was very late, even though she had known he would not get back as soon as usual, with the sheriff being absent. She suddenly made up her mind that she could wait no longer: she had to know what was keeping him.

Reaching for her coat, she heard a knock at the door. When she opened it she saw a man standing there. Dimly she made out his features in the light cast from inside the house. Her heart seemed to stop beating.

'What's wrong? Has something happened to Titus?'

'You don't know me, ma'am, but. . . .'

'You're Mr Arkwright,' she butted in. 'Tell me what's happened.'

'It's the deputy, ma'am. He's been shot.'

'Dead?'

Her flesh went cold as she waited for his answer.

'I'm right sorry, ma'am.'

'Where is he?'

'We took him back to the jailhouse.'

She closed the door and hurried past him, buttoning her coat as she broke into a run, heading for the sheriff's office. Farley Arkwright had trouble keeping pace with her as he followed.

The Deputy's Wife

'There's nothing you can do, ma'am,' he called after her.

When she reached the stoop outside the office she leapt towards the door and almost hurled herself inside. Busby Gawber was seated behind the sheriff's desk, talking with Doc Hanson. The two men turned their eyes sharply to face her as she rushed in. She looked at the doctor.

'Where is he?'

He moved towards her. 'I'm sorry, Mrs Urquart, but there was nothing I could do for him.'

'Where is he?' she almost shouted.

'He's on a cot, back in the cell area.'

She pushed past him and went into the dimly lit corridor behind the desk. Titus was lying on the cot in the second cell. Her sudden entry roused Duane Jenkins again. He eased himself up to see who had burst in at that late hour. He recognized his former wife and watched as she sank to her knees and looked at the face of her husband, his eyes closed in death.

Jenkins gazed in silence as her head lowered onto Urquart's chest and a hand rested on his forehead. She began to sob quietly, her tears mingling with the drying blood on her dead husband's shirt.

She remained on her knees for all of ten minutes, while Duane Jenkins sank back and rested his head on the pillow Urquart had earlier found for him. This was not the time to acquaint Wilhelmina with his presence or offer his condolences. Time enough for that when he was well enough to walk and ride again. She needed grieving time, but once she had adjusted to being alone again, then he would move in, offering her sympathy and a fresh start.

The sheriff was close to exhaustion when he reined the dappled grey outside Doc Hanson's abode. He almost fell from the saddle as his right leg slid over the horse's haunches. Stumbling to the front door, he leant against it as he hammered with his clenched fist. He gave the medic time to wake from his slumber before he hammered on the door again.

'I'm coming!'

When the door opened Nazeby eased himself carefully inside. 'He shot me in the arm, Doc. It's bled a lot.'

Hanson moved to aid him. 'Put your other arm round my shoulder. Let's get you into surgery.'

Twenty minutes later, the wound clean and bandaged, Doc Hanson asked himself if he should wait until daybreak before informing the sheriff what had happened in his absence. Nazeby was in no fit condition to do anything about it until after he had rested.

'Why don't you sleep in my spare room tonight, Kirk? Looks to me as if you're about all in.'

'Thanks. Doc. I'd appreciate that.'

'Come along then, I'll give you a hand.'

The sheriff had told him nothing since his first statement. He spoke again as he lowered himself onto the bed. 'You'll find Winchmore's body slung over his pinto.'

'Don't worry about him. I'll go out and take a look after we've gotten you settled.'

Tod Hanson pulled off the sheriff's boots and lifted his legs up onto the bed. He covered him with a sheet and a blanket as Nazeby closed his eyes to shut out the events of the last few hours.

Hanson went out to the horses standing quietly, ground reined near his front door. He counted his blessings. It was not often that his sleep was disturbed and, even though he had only been in slumberland for a few minutes, there was no anger in him. His thoughts sped back to Wilhelmina Urquart. He had escorted her back to her home after her weeping was over. She was numb with grief and he promised to call on her again in the morning.

'What a night,' he said out loud.

He lifted Philip Winchmore's body from the pinto and carried it inside. It could lie there on the couch until Lew Pitchley could collect it in the morning. He guessed that when the two women stood beside their husband's graves, Celeste would not be nearly as devastated as the deputy's widow.

SIXTEEN

Despite having his rest disturbed, Doc Tod Hanson's body clock awoke him as usual at 6.30 that Saturday morning. He got up, washed and dressed, then raked out the ashes from the stove. He pushed in paper and kindling wood and put a match to them. Soon the fire was blazing well and he put on coffee to heat. Only then did he look in on the sheriff.

Nazeby was sitting up on the edge of the bed. He made eye contact questioningly.

'Feeling better, Kirk?'

'Arm has stiffened up and my throat feels like a sawmill.'

'I've gotten the coffee on. I'll take a look at your arm after I've been over to your place to get you a clean shirt. I'd lend you one of mine but they're all too small.'

'You'll need the key. It's in my coat pocket.'

Hanson nodded. 'Right. Be back in ten minutes.'

The street was silent as he walked to the sheriff's living quarters next to the jailhouse. When he came out again, Busby Gawber emerged from the sheriff's office.

'Mornin', Doc.' He looked at the shirt and coat draped over Hanson's arm. 'What you got there?'

'Sheriff got back just after midnight. Shirt he was wearing was soaked with blood. Winchmore shot him in the arm. Have you been in there all night?'

'Yeah. We figured one of us should be here in case Nazeby did come back. Didn't want him t'find the body without some kind o' warnin'. He's over at your place then, is he?'

'He is. You think you could get him some breakfast from Velda and bring it over?'

'Sure, I can do that. You told him about Titus?'

'Not yet. He was tuckered out last night. He'd lost a lot of blood and he was in shock.'

'Shock?'

Hanson offered him a half smile. 'Not many folks realize, Busby, but any gunshot wound is a shock to the system and it lasts for several hours. There was nothing the sheriff could do last night anyway, so there was no point in adding to his problems. You know more about what happened than I do, so you can tell him when you bring his breakfast.'

'I'll get the keys an' lock up here. Somebody'll have t'feed Jenkins as well.'

'See you soon then.'

When Hanson got back to his house the coffee pot was boiling and he poured some into two mugs, taking one to Nazeby. 'Come into the surgery when you've gotten that down you and I'll take a look at that arm.'

Busby Gawber arrived just as the doc finished rebandaging the sheriff's wound.

'Get that down you, Sheriff, then I'll bring you up to date with what's been happening while you were gone.'

'I don't like the sound of that, Busby, but I'm famished, so don't tell me until I've cleaned this plate.'

He sat perfectly still after Gawber had finished his account, the news having shocked him temporarily into immobility. After a while he looked from Gawber to the medic and asked, 'How's Wilhelmina taking it?'

Hanson replied. 'Badly.'

'I'd best go and see her, but first I need to go and attend to Duane Jenkins. He's my responsibility until he's well enough to be moved.' He looked up at Gawber. 'You had any sleep, Busby?'

'A few hours, but them cell cots ain't much of a substitute for my bed. I'd best get back. Farley promised t'relieve me.'

'I'll come down with you. Think you could inform Lew Pitchley about Winchmore?'

'Sure, I'll do that on my way home. Here's your keys, Sheriff.'

Nazeby stared down at Titus Urquart's body and felt an emotion he could not recall having experienced before. He had seen many dead men in his time, but none of them had meant much to him. In this case he felt he had lost someone very close. Titus had been like a younger brother and the pain he felt was worse than his wound was giving him.

Then anger took hold of him. He didn't believe that Zeph Minshull had fired two shots after Titus had shot him first. He went back into his office and, handicapped though he was with his left arm in a sling, he managed to buckle his gunbelt around his hips. Farley Arkwright watched as Nazeby spun the chamber of his Colt pistol, checking that he had five bullets in it and one empty slot on which to rest the hammer. He pushed it into the holster.

'I'll be back shortly, Farley. Take those eating utensils back to Velda's when Jenkins has finished.'

'Will do, Sheriff.'

As Nazeby walked towards the hotel, Lew Pitchley arrived at the jailhouse to collect the body of Titus Urquart.

Zeph Minshull was settling his right arm in the sling Doc Hanson had advised him to use to ease the strain on his shoulder when he looked out of his bedroom window and saw the sheriff come into view. Minshull had reconciled himself to the possibility that the sheriff might arrest him, but if it did come to a trial he would plead self-defence and there was not a single witness to prove otherwise. No jury would convict him.

He walked down the hotel stairs, intent on getting breakfast. The sheriff halted in front of him as he reached ground level.

'You shot my deputy last night, Minshull.' Nazeby noticed that the killer was unarmed, so there was no immediate need to draw his own gun to emphasize his words. 'You're under arrest.'

'I was just going into the diner to have breakfast, Sheriff. Why don't you join me?'

'I've already eaten. I'll get you fed after I get you down to the jailhouse and you've answered my questions.'

Minshull shrugged with resignation. 'If you insist.'

'I do. You want to get anything from your room before we go?'

'My coat. Don't suppose you'll be detaining me for long.'

'Don't bank on it.'

Nazeby was still convinced that Minshull had shot Urquart before he had a chance to draw his own gun, even after his questioning. Minshull had been excessively polite, knowing the sheriff could never make the charge stick, unless the jury were biased.

'I'm sorry, Sheriff, but your deputy left me no choice.'

'You're a liar, Minshull.'

'Prove it.'

'We'll let a jury decide. You're under arrest for murder. Head for the cells.'

Again Minshull shrugged with resignation, his confidence still high. Nazeby put him in a cell as far away from Duane Jenkins as they could get. Then he went along to Jenkins and told him that Doc Hanson would be along later to take a look at his wounds.

Jenkins nodded. 'Looks like that Winchmore got lucky, Sheriff.'

'Not lucky enough. He's dead.'

He turned and went back into his office. 'You want I should swear you in as my deputy, Farley?'

'No, thanks, Sheriff. I'm not cut out to be a lawman, but I'll help out for as long as you need me.'

'You got somebody looking after the livery for you?'

'All fixed.'

'Good. I'm going to see Mrs Urquart.'

She looked awful as she invited him in.

'What can I say, Wil?'

'Nothing. Whatever you say won't bring him back. Have you arrested that man who shot him?'

'I have and he'll go on trial, but I don't fancy our chances of getting a conviction. No witnesses.'

She slumped dejectedly into a chair and he lowered himself to sit across from her. 'I understand the burial will be tomorrow,' he said.

When she made no response he asked, 'Anything I can do, Wil?'

She looked at him steadily for a full minute before answering.

'I might need a shoulder to lean on at the grave-side.'

'I'll come down for you.'

He was a little surprised that she had not commented on the sling supporting his left arm, but as the thought came to him she noticed it.

'You hurt bad, Sheriff?'

'No. Bullet went straight through. Clean wound.'

'And Philip Winchmore?'

'It was him or me, Wil. His luck ran out.' He got to his feet. 'I'd best go and see Celeste. I'm not looking forward to it. She's gonna hate me for the rest of her days.'

'No, I don't think so. Their's was never a love match. She married him for security and nothing else. She'll inherit the store.' Her words dried up for only a few seconds. 'What will I inherit, Sheriff?'

'Not much, I guess, apart from a roof over your head.'

After he had departed, Wilhelmina sat quietly reflecting on her fate. Her first husband had been a cheating liar who had got himself arrested and sent to jail: her second had been a loving, thoughtful man who had brought stability into her life. Now he was dead and she had nothing left to live for. Misery folded its crippling arms around her . . . until another thought came.

She went to a drawer in her dressing-table, pulled aside the clean underwear, and pulled out the derringer pistol Duane Jenkins had given her when first they were married.

His words came back to her across the years. 'I'll be away at times, Wil, and you need to be able to protect yourself. I'll teach you how to use it.'

She hadn't touched it since she had brought it

126

from her old home into the one Titus had provided for them. It felt strange to be holding it again after all those years, but as she handled it carefully she came to a decision. She would take it down to Jay Nairn and ask him to check it over and make sure it was still in good working order. The bullets were still at the back of the drawer and she took out the box. She wondered if they were too old to be used?

SEVENTEEN

The two funerals took place on Sunday morning, one prior to morning worship at the Episcopalian church, the second immediately afterwards. Celeste Winchmore was surprised that so many people followed Philip's coffin so early in the morning, which at least proved their sympathies were with her rather than the released outlaw he had attempted to kill. It lifted her spirits. In spite of the fact she had never felt love for Philip, he had been a good provider and the relationship between him and daughter Chloe had been a loving one. The child would miss her father far more than her mother would. Celeste's heart remained with the incapacitated Duane Jenkins, even if he had rejected her offer to nurse him.

Sheriff Kirk Nazeby did not go to church that morning and neither did Wilhelmina Urquart. The two of them shared coffee in her modest home before walking side by side behind the coffin, followed by what seemed like half the town. She was glad to see how much Titus had been respected, but

128

would their sympathies extend through the lonely days that stretched ahead of her? Words of condolence were offered to her as she was escorted back home by the sheriff, after the minister had mouthed his customary speech of hope about the resurrection to eternal life, and the coffin had been lowered into the ground.

Emptiness robbed her of all desire for food or drink after the sheriff had left her and she took to her bed. She dozed fitfully and the hours were divided between a numbing consciousness and the merciful relief of sleep.

Even the saloons were quiet for the remainder of that day, apart from the few patrons who drowned their sorrows in drink. For those who had any connection with the recent deaths, the hours dragged slowly.

Nazeby was comforted by the magnanimous attitude that Celeste Winchmore had taken. She had even apologized for her late husband having wounded him. It reminded him of how much he wanted to throw away the sling and exercise his stiffened arm.

He had a late lunch in Velda's eating-house but hardly tasted a thing.

'Was that all right, Sheriff?'

'Fine, Velda, just fine,' he replied self-consciously. 'Send in your bill for feeding my prisoner. Make out a separate one for Duane Jenkins. He's not under arrest, so he'll have to pay for his own feeding.'

'What's going to happen to him, Sheriff?'

'As soon as he's fit to move again he'll have to find a bed in the hotel. He was taken to the jailhouse for his own protection, but I reckon any threat to his life has gone now.'

Busby Gawber took over the night shift at the jailhouse, happy to earn a few dollars at the taxpayers' expense. He eked out a living odd-jobbing, and playing night guard was as easy as any other task.

Doc Hanson had a quiet day, apart from dressing the wounds of Duane Jenkins, Zeph Minshull and Sheriff Nazeby. He, as much as anyone else, had his mind on the trial that would face Minshull when the circuit judge arrived in town three days later. With nothing more than supposition for evidence, his chances of being found not guilty were good. There were a few hotheads in favour of dragging Minshull from his cell and having a lynching party, but everybody knew the sheriff would not stand for that. His gun hand was still in good working order and he would shoot any man that tried to rob him of his prisoner. He would also stand by whatever verdict the jury brought in after the trial. A sense of gloom had its effect on everyone concerned and patience quickly began to wear thin. Nazeby felt sick with defeat, even before that first day of waiting for the trial had ended. He took to his bed with a pessimism which was foreign to him.

The following day Celeste Winchmore threw herself into the task of learning all about her late husband's business, while Quenella Revett found the widow's lack of need for grieving time almost repellent. Quenella's relationship with the dead man had always been a cordial one and it seemed to her that she would miss him far more than his widow.

Celeste served customers with a smile on her face. Many of them looked around in the store as much out of morbid curiosity than the need to make purchases. The contact with so many people pushed Philip to the back of her mind.

She had been pleasantly surprised to learn that the undertaker had found more than $10,000 in her husband's pockets and saddle-bags, which she had immediately deposited in the bank. In a practical sense she had no worries for the future. With the income from the store and her bank assets her financial position was far better than she could have expected.

Meanwhile, Wilhelmina Urquart roused herself from lethargy, slowly becoming aware that allowing herself to wallow in misery was an attitude of defeatism. Had it been she who had been killed, Titus would have been positive about it, even though she knew he would have been devastated by his loss. She owed it to him to make sure his killer did not escape the due punishment for his crime.

She washed and dressed, forced food and drink into her mouth, then put on her bonnet and coat and went to see Jay Nairn.

His face was sombre as he offered her his condolences. 'We'll all miss him, Mrs Urquart. Titus was a fine man.'

131

'Yes, he was, Mr Nairn, and I appreciate how much people respected him.'

'So what can I do for you, Mrs Urquart?'

She pulled the derringer from her coat pocket and handed it to him. 'I've had this little gun a long time, but I haven't used it in more than five years, so I thought I'd best let you take a look at it to see if it's still safe to use. I've got some ammunition, too, but I'm not sure if it's still usable.'

'Is this the gun Duane Jenkins bought for you when you were first married?'

'It is, yes. I might have to fall back on it for protection again now, so. . . .'

'Of course. Let's go out the back and I'll try it out.'

She followed him as he checked the mechanism. 'Needs a touch of oil, Mrs Urquart, before I load it. It's gone stiff through lack of use. No rust on it though.'

Just two drops of oil and repeated operation eased the stiffness and he put in one of her old bullets. It fired perfectly and when he examined the remainder of her shells he found nothing wrong with them.

'When did you buy these? Five or six years ago?'

'About that. I used to practise target shooting quite a lot before I married Titus.'

He put in another shell and handed her the derringer. 'Try it now and let's see how good your aim is. Aim at six o'clock on that target. It's twenty yards away, so don't expect to hit bull.'

She raised her hand and extended her arm, then squeezed the trigger quickly and smoothly, just the

132

way Duane Jenkins had taught her to do. The bullet hit just to the left of twelve o'clock on the target, which surprised the gunsmith.

'That was pretty good from that distance. Derringers are not usually very effective from so far away. You wouldn't have killed an attacker, but it would have given him a nasty bite.'

'I don't expect I'd be thinking of shooting a man who was twenty yards away from me, Mr Nairn. Duane only bought it for me to protect myself from attack while he was away.'

'Of course. You want to go closer and get the feel of it again?'

It was an opportunity too inviting to pass up. She knew that Titus had constantly honed his skills with his Smith & Wesson and it seemed only wise for her to do the same with the derringer.

'May I?'

'Of course. Take as long as you like. I'll be inside when you're through.'

He left her, thinking the practice might take her mind off her grief. But he couldn't help wondering why she had felt the need so soon after burying Titus.

EIGHTEEN

Dollar bills floated in Zeph Minshull's mind's eye and helped to disperse the niggling doubts about his decision to stay and face trial for shooting the deputy. He did wonder if it would have been wiser to run after Doc Hanson had dressed his wound on the night of the shooting, but now it was too late. That option was no longer open to him. He knew it was that second shot he had fired which condemned him in the eyes of the sheriff. Had he fired only the once, then his story would hold more credence, but at the time he had wanted to make sure he had done what he set out to do. It was futile to speculate which of his two shots had been the fatal one. Maybe the first would have been enough, but that was something he would never know. He had been lucky that Urquart was dying when he fired his own gun, otherwise his aim would have likely been more precise. What irony that would have been: getting himself buried alongside the deputy for a thousand dollars he could never receive.

Judge Stevenson alighted from the night train just before ten o'clock on Wednesday. Sheriff Nazeby was there to meet him.

'Howdy, Kirk. You got any business for me tomorrow?'

'Just the one case, Judge. My deputy was murdered last Friday night.'

'Urquart? How did that happen?'

The sheriff outlined what had occurred in his absence as he escorted the judge to the hotel, where his room for the night had been reserved. After the judge had signed the register, the two men climbed the stairs to his room in silence. A bottle of whiskey and two glasses had been brought up on a tray by prior arrangement. The judge uncorked the bottle and poured for the both of them. He eyed the sheriff sombrely as he sat down.

'You think you'll get a conviction?'

'That's what half the town wants, never mind me.'

'With a rigged jury?'

Nazeby's eyes blazed anger. 'You should know me better than that by now, Judge!'

'I thought I did, but you're looking at this case through clouds of hate, Kirk. There are no witnesses, so how can any honest jury convict this man? All you've got is supposition and in a court of law that's not enough.'

The furrows on Nazeby's forehead deepened. 'Are you saying I should forget the whole thing and let

135

this killer go free?'

'You can bring him up before me if you like, if it's a case of saving face and pacifying the townsfolk, but I can tell you now, unless you can put up a better case than you've just outlined to me, I shall have no option but to dismiss the case for lack of evidence. I can't leave it for the jury to decide.'

'I've had him locked up since Saturday morning, Judge, I have to put him on trial.'

'In that case, I'll see you in court. Goodnight, Sheriff.'

Nazeby was being dismissed abruptly and he knew it. Whenever Judge Stevenson called him by his title instead of his given name he was being officious. The sheriff emptied his whiskey glass and departed without another word.

His normal placid equilibrium deserted him as he walked back to the jailhouse for a final check before returning to his living quarters for the night. He looked at a seemingly confident Zeph Minshull with hatred in his heart and it showed in his eyes.

'Somebody upset you, Sheriff?' Minshull asked casually.

Nazeby turned away and walked along the corridor to the cell where Duane Jenkins was recumbent on the cot. When he had the outlaw's attention he said, 'Doc Hanson tells me you're fit enough to get on your feet now, so I've booked you a room at the hotel. I'll escort you over there after breakfast.'

'Thanks, Sheriff. You're gettin' mighty considerate in your old age.'

As he turned away, Nazeby suddenly did feel old. He brushed a hand through his prematurely white hair and scratched an itch. He glared at Busby Gawber as he came through into the office.

'Have I done somethin' wrong, Sheriff?'

Nazeby took a grip on himself, realizing he had allowed his emotions to make him lose control. He sighed heavily and forced a half smile. 'No, Busby, I'm not mad at you.'

He picked up his hat and said, 'See you in the morning.'

The trial took no more than ten minutes before Judge Stevenson dismissed the case for lack of evidence, to the consternation of those who had come to see Zeph Minshull convicted of murder. The judge banged his gavel ferociously and called for order. It took more than a minute for the rebellious crowd to quiet down, then the judge told Minshull, 'You're free to go.'

He turned his attention to the sheriff. 'Sheriff, if any threats are made against the acquitted man, I'll hold you responsible for his safety. This is a court of law and my judgment is not an excuse for a hanging party.'

Nazeby turned to face the assembly. 'Clear the court! Quietly now. You heard what the judge said.'

One of the first to leave was Wilhelmina Urquart. Her hope of seeing her husband's killer convicted had been a slim one, but now even that had turned to ashes.

Zeph Minshull was visibly shaking when the last man went out and the sheriff turned back to him.

'What are you gonna do, Sheriff? That crowd sounds like a lynchin' party t'me.'

'They know as well as I do, Minshull, that you're as guilty as hell. You've gotten off on a technicality, just like you expected all along. Don't look to me for sympathy.'

'It's your job t'protect me!'

'And I'll do that. If need be I'll put you back in that cell for your own protection, but only until nightfall. After that you're on your own. I'd advise you to skip town and ride as far away as you can, you bastard.'

Judge Stevenson, standing only a few yards away, chose to ignore what the sheriff had said to Minshull as he came closer. He spoke quietly. 'Do you think I might need your protection before I take the train out of Eden, Sheriff?'

Zeph Minshull accepted the protection he had been offered. He had travelled light and there was nothing left of his at the hotel.

'You can stay here until after dark, like I told you,' the sheriff informed him, 'but you pay your hotel tab first.'

'I can't go over there, Sheriff!'

'Then give me some money and I'll pay it for you. I'll get you a receipt.'

Minshull dived into a pocket and handed over

more than he felt he owed. 'I could use the change,' he said.

With the judge gone on his journey, Nazeby went back to the jailhouse to release Minshull. 'I'd wait another hour if I were you. There'll still be men on the streets, drifting home in twos and threes. I've told Farley Arkwright to leave the livery doors closed but unlocked, in case I want my horse. But watch yourself. You're responsible for your own neck from now on.'

An hour later Busby Gawber, sworn to secrecy by the sheriff, let Minshull out by the rear door. Minshull made his way towards the livery stables, looking back several times to see if he was being followed. He saw no one. Having to leave Eden without the thousand dollars Jenkins had promised irritated him intensely, but life was still more important to him than money. A man could always get money if he was prepared to be ruthless and take a few risks.

Across the street a short figure with hat pulled well down and hands in the pockets of a heavy coat that seemed at least two sizes too large, observed Minshull enter the stables, then crossed the street quickly. The watcher crept inside on cat-soft feet. Just one lantern burned inside, revealing the killer busy with bridle and saddle. He turned as the intruder moved towards him and pushed the hat well back.

His hands ceased to move as he recognized the face beneath abundant black hair. 'You! What the hell are you doing here?'

'You got away with murder, and all because the judge's hands were tied by the law, only my hands are free to do whatever I want with them.'

He stared as the gun appeared, as if by magic, held two-handed and aimed at his chest, no more than four feet away. There was an explosion as the trigger was squeezed and Zeph Minshull felt the impact, just before his heart ceased to beat and he crumpled in a heap alongside his mount's front feet.

The short figure pulled the hat down low again and quietly slipped away.

NINETEEN

Farley Arkwright pushed open the door of Velda's eating-house and saw the sheriff sitting at a table, having breakfast. Farley ambled forward, breathing heavily, and sat down opposite Nazeby.

'Been running, Farley? You'll have to watch it, at your age.'

Arkwright said nothing until his breathing returned close to normal, while the sheriff carried on eating as he waited for the momentous news he knew the liveryman was eager to impart. Nazeby forked another portion of fried egg.

'You enjoying that, Sheriff?'

'Best meal of the day, I always say, breakfast. Mind you, having to use a fork in my right hand, what with having a damaged wing, slows me down a bit. Will it wait 'til I've finished?'

'Will what wait?'

Nazeby's eyebrows contracted. 'You didn't get yourself all out of' – he forked a piece of ham this time – 'breath just because you yearned for my company. Somebody stole my horse, have they?'

'No. Your grey is fine, as far as I know. I haven't started feeding yet.'

'It's still early.'

Curiosity was having a battle in the sheriff's mind with his desire to enjoy his food, and food won.

After he had cleared his plate and reached for the coffee Velda's assistant was pouring for him, he decided he could wait no longer for the news. 'All right, Farley, I reckon I'm ready for the shock.'

'I hope so.' He paused ominously. 'Somebody shot Minshull.'

'Dead?'

'As a dodo.'

Nazeby didn't know whether to smile or frown. He was glad to hear the man was dead, but he did not fancy the investigation he would be obliged to make into the killing. There were too many men who had wanted Minshull to hang and he had no idea where to start. He sipped his coffee contemplatively.

'That makes three coffins for Lew Pitchley in a week. He'll start to wonder if it's celebration time.'

'And you'll have to try and find out who did it.'

Nazeby drained his cup and stood up, adjusting the sling supporting his left arm. 'Lead on, Farley. Best get started.'

The hole in Minshull's chest was small and the bullet was still in his chest. Nazeby concluded it had been fired from a small calibre gun. 'That might narrow down the suspects,' he said.

142

'Do me a favour, Doc?'

'Anything that's legal, Sheriff.'

'Dig out that bullet. I need to know what calibre gun fired it. The killer could be a gambling man.'

'A derringer, you mean?'

'It's a possibility, but I'm only guessing.'

'Visitors already,' Duane Jenkins said in surprise.

'Visitor, singular,' the sheriff corrected.

'And to what do I owe the pleasure, so soon after breakfast?'

'I've gotten news for you, Jenkins, though I'm not sure if you'll be glad or not.'

They eyed each other through a long silence, until Jenkins lost his patience. 'Well spit it out then! Who's dead now?'

'Why should anybody be dead?'

'Well a raid on the bank don't concern me an' I can't imagine your news has anything t'do with Wil?'

'No, nothing to do with your ex-wife. But you're right, somebody is dead.' He paused to give emphasis to the revelation he was about to make. 'It's Zeph Minshull.'

Jenkins felt his heart skip with joy. Now his own implication as an accessory before the fact of Deputy Urquart's murder could never be revealed. He managed to look surprised. 'Zeph?'

'Zeph.'

'How come?'

'Happened late last night. He'd decided to leave town quietly, but somebody must have guessed what he had in mind and kept watch on him. He was shot as he was saddling his horse.'

The response came without Jenkins having to give it prior consideration. 'Wouldn't have been you, would it?'

'I'd had him in protective custody all day.' He saw no reason to refute the accusation or to inform Jenkins that he had already gone to bed by the time Minshull left the jailhouse. 'I didn't want a lynching party on my hands.'

'Well, if it wasn't you, Nazeby, who was it?'

'I thought you might be able to point me in that direction. You knew him better than anybody else in town. The two of you were friends, by your own admission. And his.'

Jenkins shook his head. 'Can't help you, Sheriff. Like you, I assume, I was asleep. The doc gave me laudanum to ease the pain in my chest last night.'

'You don't know anybody who might have followed him to Eden? Somebody with a grudge?'

'Hell, Sheriff, I hadn't seen the man for ten years, 'til he showed up last week.'

'Oh, well, it made an excuse to come and see how you were doing. Looking after you all right, are they?'

'As if you care. But just to satisfy your curiosity, the doc says I can walk around the room, preferably every hour, just to get my legs goin' again. They've stiffened up real bad, especially the left one that took

144

the bullet. Can't stand my weight on it yet. In another few days I should be out an' about, usin' those crutches t'take gentle exercise, an' sharing a beer with old friends. You might be surprised, but there are men in Eden who will still talk t'me.'

'I'm not surprised, Duane. After all, your crimes were all committed well away from Eden. Folks are funny that way. So long as they're not the losers they don't give a damn.'

With no leads to the killer, Nazeby sought the aid of Jay Nairn.

'Who do you know has small calibre weapons, Jay?'

Nairn put forward a dozen names, then said, 'But I don't see any of them killing that drifter, Kirk.'

'A lot of folks respected Titus Urquart and wanted to see his killer hang, Jay. When he didn't, somebody decided to rectify the injustice.'

'I don't see no tears in your eyes. You're quite sure it was murder then?'

'Absolutely. Not a single doubt in my mind.'

'Well. . . .' Nairn sighed. 'Seems to me you've about as much chance of finding Minshull's killer as . . .'

'The proverbial needle in the haystack,' the sheriff concluded for him.

'You tell fortunes, too, Kirk?'

Duane Jenkins followed Doc Hanson's advice with almost meticulous care and, four weeks after having been shot, the wound in his thigh had healed completely, as had the one in his side. He had discarded the crutches. Farley Arkwright had been exercising his horse for him two or three times a week, but now Jenkins decided he was ready to get back into the saddle himself.

'Short rides at first,' Doc Hanson advised, 'and no loping. The horse might need it but you don't. You need another two weeks before your chest will stand up to fast riding.'

He resisted the urge to call on Celeste Winchmore during the evenings, after she had put Chloe to bed. Celeste had called at the hotel and repeated her invitation for him to convalesce in his old home but, in spite of being sorely tempted, he had pointed out that it would harm her reputation.

'I don't care about my reputation. I've lost Philip, but I don't want to lose you as well.'

She didn't seem to realize the depth of her own infatuation and the harm it could bring her.

'You'd become a scarlet woman, just for me?'

Her shoulders lifted and fell dismissively. 'Folks will talk, even about the innocent.'

'You've gotten a living to make with that store, Celeste. If I came to live with you, half the town would boycott your place an' go elsewhere for supplies an' clothing.'

She shrugged again. 'They'd forget about us in a week.'

'No, they wouldn't. Besides, Doc Hanson has put a ban on sexual intercourse for at least six weeks,' he lied easily.

'Doctors don't know everything, Duane.'

He laughed softly. 'You're one helluva woman, Celeste, but I think it would be best t'foller his advice. When the time is up an' I'm feelin' fit an' frisky again, who knows?'

The six weeks were up and he *was* feeling fit and frisky again. Doc Hanson had pronounced him fully healed, no longer in need of medical attention, and he was back to riding out into open country, letting the gelding with the two front white socks stretch his legs in fast gallops. But it was not Celeste Winchmore who occupied his thoughts. Titus Urquart was dead and buried and Wilhelmina was alone again. He had been disappointed that she had not even felt the desire to call and see him. By now she must surely be needing a man, in more ways than one. Urquart had not left her more than a few dollars, according to the information Jenkins had received.

Time to pay her a visit.

TWENTY

He knocked on her door and waited. It was a full minute before she came and opened it.

'What kept you?' she asked cynically.

'I've been nursin' gunshot wounds, Wil, or hadn't you heard?' he replied with a note of sarcasm. 'Can I come in?'

She stood aside and, after he had passed her, she closed the door and followed him.

He turned to face her. 'How are you copin', Wil?'

'Same way most women cope after they've lost their husbands. I'm watching the pennies.'

'You must be nigh on broke by now. Urquart didn't leave you much, did he?'

'How would you know?'

'I have ways of findin' out these things.'

She did not invite him to sit and remained standing herself.

'How are you spendin' your time now?' he asked her.

She walked over to the sideboard and picked up

the derringer pistol she had been practising with earlier. 'Remember this?'

'You kept it all these years?' he said in surprise. 'I'd have thought the deputy would've told you t'get rid of it.'

'The deputy never knew I had it. I've kept it hidden ever since I married him. Now I've started practising with it again.'

'Can you still hit a target?'

She lifted it and aimed it at his heart. He was not wearing his gunbelt, she had noticed. 'You sure you want to find out?'

'Put it down, Wil. We don't want no accidents.'

She lowered the pistol but retained it in her right hand.

'What did you come for, Duane?'

'T'see how you are.'

'Is that all?'

'Er . . . no. I figured that now you're alone again, maybe we could start over.'

'Whatever gave you that idea?'

It registered in his mind that she had not offered him even the vestige of a smile since he had arrived. Through those long years in prison it was her smile that had kept him going, hoping to win her back once he was free again.

'It's not good for a woman t'live alone, Wil, an' you especially. You're still young an' even more beautiful than you were when we married. You've blossomed, sweetheart.'

'I'm no longer your sweetheart.'

'But you could be, startin' right now. I'll take good care o' you, Wil.'

Her lips curled in a sneer of contempt. 'Oh, no, you won't. That man who murdered Titus was a friend of yours, and' – her voice rose to a crescendo – 'he did it on your instructions!'

'Wil! How can you say that?'

'What possible other reason could there be? I talked it over with Titus and we decided you only stayed on in Eden because of me. He was no fool. He knew you wanted me back and the only way you had a chance of that was to see him dead first.'

He started to protest his innocence. 'That ain't so.'

She cut him short. 'You planned to pick a fight with him. You went out of town each day to practise your fast draw.'

His eyebrows lifted as he moved his head from side to side in denial. 'You've got it all wrong, Wil.'

'Oh, no, I haven't. Even the sheriff knew what you were up to; he told me after Titus had been buried. But then you got shot yourself, so you had your old buddy do the job for you. I'm not stupid, Duane, and neither is the sheriff. We know you told that Minshull to shoot first, before Titus had a chance to defend himself. You both worked it out that if he pleaded self-defence, with no witnesses to dispute his claim, he'd get away with it. But I fixed him, didn't I?'

She revelled in his stare of astonishment. 'You!?'

'Yes, Duane, me! One shot, straight to the heart, so now you have your answer ... I *can* hit a target, plumb centre.'

150

Their eyes locked as he digested a side of her he had not suspected. 'An' Nazeby's been goin' round in circles lookin' for Zeph's killer. He'd never suspect a nice girl like you, would he?'

'That's right, he wouldn't. I'm still the angelic wife of his late deputy, and he wouldn't suspect me of killing you, either, if I could do it in a safe place.'

His gaze clearly indicated he could not believe what she was telling him. He smiled broadly. His smile had always been able to charm away any disgruntled feelings she had. 'That's foolish talk, Wil. You'd never shoot me.'

She lifted the derringer again while he continued to stare at her, still telling himself that this woman had once loved him to distraction and would again.

'I knew you'd come for me one day and I've been waiting for you, Duane. Minshull is dead and now it's your turn.'

For the first time he began to take her seriously. 'You'd never get away with it, Wil. They'd hang you, an' you know it.'

He thought of jumping her, but she was standing a good six feet away from him. He didn't want another bullet in his chest.

'Go up to the bedroom,' she commanded.

'The bedroom?'

'That's what I said.'

He smiled at her again. So that was it. This was all horseplay. She had been a very passionate girl in the two years they had lived together and now her physical needs had reached a pitch of desperation. She was going to seduce him. He could barely believe his luck.

He climbed the narrow staircase, thinking what a fool he'd been to take her threat seriously. She still had feelings for him, after all these years.

'Turn around,' she commanded, after she followed him into the bedroom. When he turned he saw that the derringer was again pointing at his heart.

'There's no need for all this dramatic stuff, Wil. I'll gladly submit.'

She was disgusted by the implication of his bantering words, but dismissed them in favour of practicalities.

'You're wrong. Duane, they won't hang me. I'll tell the sheriff you tried to rape me. He'll put me on trial, but what jury would convict a woman defending her honour?'

The pressure of her trigger finger sent the bullet straight into his heart. He fell against the bed and slowly subsided. How ironic, she thought. What Philip Winchmore had failed to do with three Winchester rifle bullets, she had accomplished with a far less lethal weapon.

She threw the gun down on the floor and clawed at her dress. By the time she had finished the bodice was ripped in two places, the skirt in three, and one sleeve was almost torn off at the shoulder. She rucked up the bed to give the impression of a struggle, mussed up her abundant black hair and looked at herself in the long mirror by the window. Now she *did* look something like a rape victim. Then she calmly walked down the stairs.

Someone rapped on the front door and it opened as she stood mesmerized. Sheriff Kirk Nazeby walked in.

'I thought I heard a shot, Wil?'

Her brain ice cold, she said quietly, her voice breaking, 'You did, Sheriff. I've just killed him. I was just coming to tell you.'

He stared at the tears in her dress. 'Killed who?'

'Duane.' She explained in a voice she had practised well, full of emotion. 'He came to ask me to go away with him and when I refused he tried to rape me. He said if he couldn't have me, no other man would.'

She lowered her head and forced a sob from her throat. He moved towards her and took her in his arms. She put her head on his shoulder and thought of Titus.

Then the tears came effortlessly.

TWENTY-ONE

As she dried her eyes she said quietly, 'Get him out of here, Sheriff. He's polluting my bedroom '

'I'll fetch Lew Pitchley to come and take him away, but let's get you out of here first.'

'Are you going to arrest me?'

'Not right now, Wil. I'll take you to stay a while with the mayor's wife. She's been quite friendly with you since. . . .'

'Yes, she has. Thank you, Sheriff.'

Lillian Openshaw, a homemaking sort of woman in her late forties, was both shocked and solicitous when Nazeby told her what happened. 'Will you look after her for awhile, Mrs Openshaw?'

'Of course I will,' she offered eagerly. 'You come and sit down, my dear. Or would you rather lie down for a little while?'

The shock of what she had done was beginning to take hold of Wilhelmina. 'Yes, I would. Thank you.'

The sheriff waited while the mayor's wife settled Wilhelmina in her own bedroom. When she returned she looked at him anxiously. 'Will you have to arrest her, Sheriff?'

'I'll talk to the mayor about that, ma'am. He's a real stickler for following the letter of the law and Wil did kill a man. But right now I need to get the body out of her house, so if you'll excuse me?'

'Of course.'

'I'll be back in about an hour.'

The sheriff helped Lew Pitchley carry the body down the stairs and load it on to his buckboard, then went off to inform Doc Hanson. Again he asked the doctor to dig out the bullet, once he had certified Duane Jenkins dead. A niggling suspicion had crept into his mind which he was anxious to disprove.

Then he went to visit the mayor in his law office. Explaining what had transpired in the Urquart home, he waited for the mayor to comment.

Segal Openshaw was a man of some fifty years, with thinning mousy hair. He was overweight through a tendency to indulge too well on his wife's cooking. He took a cigar from the box on his desk, struck a lucifer and put flame to tobacco. He puffed on it vigorously as he considered his response.

'Bad business, Sheriff, bad. Both me and my wife have been concerned about Wilhelmina since Titus was shot, but I cannot allow my sympathy to overrule my duty as a citizen, as well as mayor of Eden. You'll have to follow procedure and charge her. There are those in our town who will not excuse murder under any circumstances and that is what this is, whether we like it or not.'

'You think a jury would convict her, after what happened to my deputy? Titus was held in high regard by most folks, and Wil was only defending herself against a man who wanted to rape her.'

'Only the trial will answer that question. If my wife is agreeable, you can leave her with us until the trial. I'll be responsible for her appearance in court. No need for you to put her in that jail of yours. Be almost another month before Judge Stevenson comes again.'

Nazeby was pleased with the mayor's offer. He would have found it both hurtful and embarrassing to have to confine Wilhelmina Urquart in one of his cells. 'I'll take a full statement from her as soon as she's up to it and get her to sign it, while it's all still fresh in her mind.'

'You do that, then you can produce it in court, if necessary.'

Nazeby went back to Lew Pitchley's funeral parlour before returning to see Wilhelmina. Lew eyed him with a troubled look. 'You'll find the bullet in that little dish over there, Sheriff.'

Nazeby found it significant that Pitchley used his title in preference to his forename and that, coupled with that anxiety-riddled gaze, worried him. He went over and picked up the bullet, then held it up to the light to take a closer look.

Judge Stevenson had never liked having women brought up before him, but he was not going to allow that fact to influence the way in which he conducted the trial. If she was found guilty of murder she would hang, the same as a man.

As everyone had anticipated, the accused admitted killing her first husband, but pleaded self-defence. Sheriff Kirk Nazeby testified that when he entered the house after the shooting, Wilhelmina Urquart's dress was badly torn – he produced the dress for the jury to see – her hair mussed, and the bedclothes in disarray, indicating a struggle between her and Duane Jenkins. She had stated that she had shot him to save herself from being raped. That was all the evidence that was available for the judge and jury to consider.

Not a single member of the jury had any liking for the dead man, but two of them would not yield to the pleading of the other ten, who were in favour of acquittal. That fact left the judge with little option but to accept the verdict of the majority.

'Let the accused rise,' the judge said after the foreman informed him of the stalemate.

The widow pushed herself erect from the hard chair.

'Wilhelmina Urquart, by a majority of ten to two, the jury feel you acted in self-defence when you shot Duane Jenkins. I hope this will not set a precedent.' He raised his eyes to encompass the whole assembly of townsfolk. 'I want everyone in this courtroom to remember that taking another life is against the law, whatever the circumstances.'

His gaze was drawn back to the woman. 'Had you accepted my offer to allow you to plead guilty to second degree murder instead of first, the jury might have come to a different conclusion. You took the risk of being sentenced to hang, had the jury found you guilty. Your faith in your fellow citizens, as well as your honour, has been vindicated. You are free to go.

'Court dismissed!'

It was not until two days later that Sheriff Nazeby visited his former deputy's widow, now back in her own home. She was pleased to see him. Since the trial she had contemplated a bleak future, alone and with no money, apart from what had been collected by Lillian Openshaw from sympathetic citizens. Those who had not donated money had provided food and her larder was filled to capacity. The possibility of a third marriage had not even entered her head.

'How are you, Wil?'

She did not look at him as she replied, 'I'm lost without Titus. I don't know what I'm going to do, Sheriff.'

'You could face another murder trial,' he said casually.

She stared back at him, shocked rigid by his statement.

'Whatever do you mean, Sheriff?' she asked. Then it dawned on her that somehow he knew.

He took two lead slugs from his pocket and held them up, one in each hand. She could not see that one of them was marked with a number one and the other with a number two.

He lifted his right hand a few inches. 'This is the bullet we took out of Duane's body.' He then raised his left hand a few inches. 'And this is the one taken from the body of Zeph Minshull. I've examined them closely, Wil. They were both fired from the same gun.'

The thought of facing another trial was more than she could bear. 'You can't prove that, Sheriff.'

'Maybe not well enough to convince a judge and jury, but I know now that it was you who killed Minshull. I've known it since the day after you killed Jenkins.'

'But. . . .'

'No buts, Wil. I don't blame you for what you did. We all know Minshull got away with murder, until you rectified that injustice, but I want you to remember for the rest of your days that I do not hold with murder. What puzzles me is how you got close enough to Minshull to do it without him killing you first, or at least going for his gun and wounding you.'

She smiled at the memory of how she had planned her act of vengeance against the man who had shot her husband. How she had worn Titus's old coat to make her look as broad as a man, and his hat, under which she could hide all that black hair in case anyone saw her lurking in the shadows. How she had crept into the livery stables and got the drop on Minshull. She had not given him the slightest chance to draw his gun, but that was something she was not going to admit.

'Somebody shot Minshull, Sheriff, but if you arrest

me and put me on trial for his killing you'll be laughed out of court.'

He knew she was right. He should have kept his suspicions to himself. The change in her attitude made him see that she wanted him gone. He had gained nothing by accusing her. The warm friendship they had shared had suddenly died.

He turned and went out through the front door, not even bothering to close it as he left.